Finding Clarity

Lisa Frieden

Copyright © 2016 Frieden Press

ISBN: 978-0-9969409-4-8

CHAPTER ONE

10:15 a.m. Friday, September, San Francisco

"Your sister's in trouble. Need your help." The text message popped up on Zoe's phone, an unknown number and an area code she didn't recognize.

Her heart skipped a beat. Was Clare in trouble?

Her eyes shot to the framed photograph on her desk next to her computer. In it, she stood with Clare on the Golden Gate Bridge, beaming for the camera, their arms slung around each other and their hair whipping in the cold wind blowing off the Pacific Ocean. It was taken six months ago in March, when she'd first arrived in San Francisco, hoping to be closer to Clare who'd left Phoenix looking for a cure for her kidney problems.

Zoe turned back to her phone. It had rung several times in the last half hour, but she'd let it go to voicemail because she'd been under deadline. Now, she scrolled down her call list. The recent calls had all come from the same number as the text message, but the person hadn't left a message.

What was going on?

1

As she reread the text, her phone came alive in her hand, vibrating, lighting up, and ringing, the same number on the screen.

"Who is this?" She spoke softly so her co-workers in the nearby cubicles wouldn't overhear.

"Shadow. I'm a friend of your sister's."

"Shadow?" She frowned. He sounded like Clare's Seeker friends, who adopted fanciful personas rather than be themselves.

Shadow kept talking. "You've got to come to Harmony and get Clarity, right away."

"Her name is 'Clare,' not 'Clarity,'" Zoe said with irritation, as she felt her anxiety level rise. "What's wrong? Is Clare OK?"

Clare's regular weekly phone calls had stopped abruptly two weeks ago. Zoe had tried not to worry. It was difficult for Clare to hitch a ride out of the remote Humboldt forest to call her, but in their last conversation, Clare had mentioned feeling tired.

"She's in danger." The man's hushed tone dropped lower, his words hurried and urgent.

"Is it her kidneys?" Zoe asked.

"Her kidneys? I don't know anything about that." The man sounded confused.

"Then what are you talking about? Is this about the Seekers?"

Clare had moved to Humboldt two months ago to join the Seekers, who she'd claimed were a peaceful group worshiping nature, marijuana and trees. Zoe looked at the photo on her desk again. Last March felt like eons ago.

"There's someone after her," the man said, "a very bad man. I've gotta—"

"Wait, what bad man?"

"I can't get into it right now."

"Let me talk to Clare!"

"She's not here."

"Where is she?"

"At Harmony. She hasn't been feeling well."

"What do you mean, not feeling well?" Panic skittered through her.

"She didn't say. You got a pen and paper? You'll need directions."

"Wait, Shadow. You say you're a friend of my sister's, but how do I know that's true? Why should I believe you?"

"Because we both want Clarity safe." Impatience vibrated through the man's voice. "Look, you're right to be suspicious, but I'm not the enemy, trust me. I wouldn't be calling if I didn't need your help. I'll tell you everything when you get here. Ready for directions?"

She didn't like being kept in the dark, but if Clare was in trouble, she had to go. She grabbed her keyboard and pulled up a blank document on her screen.

"Ready," she said.

Fear raced through her as she began typing. Who was this guy Shadow? And what bad man was he talking about? But none of that worried her as much as Clare's health. Was her sister stranded somewhere in the forest suffering kidney failure?

\#

10:30 a.m. Friday, Redway

Jason stood at the back of the grocery store parking lot in Redway, the closest town to Harmony with a decent market. He finished the call with Clarity's sister and felt relieved. The sooner Clarity was safely out of the way, the sooner he could refocus his energy on his undercover work with the Seekers and taking down Rob Heller.

He started to call his boss, but a battered white pickup pulled into the parking lot. He pocketed the burner and froze where he stood, his body blending into the shadows of the redwood forest that stood tall and dark behind him.

A burly, gray-haired man climbed out of the truck and lumbered into the store.

Derrick Hanks.

The old logger hated hippies, druggies, and pretty much everything except booze. Undoubtedly, Hanks would find the Seekers inside shopping, loading up on supplies for their commune, and he'd pick some kind of a fight. On the plus side, he'd stall them long enough for Jason to call his boss.

Jason scanned the parking area again. It was empty, except for Derrick's truck and a rusting, ancient Subaru. The tourists were long gone now that it was late September, and Friday mid-morning, most locals were at work. He glanced out at Redwood Drive, the main drag in Redway, an old lumber town just off the highway that had once seen better days. No traffic visible at all.

He pulled out the burner again.

"It's about fucking time." Trevor Porter sounded even more irritated than usual. "You were supposed to call three days ago. What the hell's going on?"

"This is the first chance I've had, sir," he said.

Jason should have known the lieutenant would go on the attack. He'd only started working for Porter six weeks ago, but it was long enough for him to learn that his boss had a short fuse and a foul mouth.

"Really? In that big fucking forest, you couldn't find the time to get the fuck away from that goddamn cult of hippies and use the goddamn sat phone?"

"It's not as easy as you think, given the conditions, sir." He didn't have time to argue the finer points of satellite phone use in rugged, densely forested terrain. "Look, I've only got a few minutes to talk, so why don't we stay on task."

"Right, so what the hell you got?"

"I've figured out who Heller's contact is with the Seekers—"

"I don't give a crap about Heller's henchmen!" Porter cut him off, his temper flaring again. "They're a dime a dozen and don't amount to jack when it comes to getting that goddamn drug dealer."

"Yes, sir." Jason clenched his teeth and tried to keep his own temper under control. "But Fox meets periodically with Heller. If I track him, I might be able to ascertain Heller's timing so we can plan the bust." He rubbed the beard he'd grown for his disguise as Shadow. The thing still felt weird.

"You've gotta deliver, Jason. I'm counting on you." Porter took a swig of his ever-present cup of coffee. "You know the fucking DEA doesn't respect us. The Feds are circling, getting ready to launch their own raid. If that happens, the our task force may as well kiss this whole goddamned investigation good-bye."

"I understand your concern, sir." Jason spoke respectfully, hoping to calm his boss.

His assignment to the task force had been a big step up from his position in the narcotics division of the San Francisco Police Department. He wasn't about to fail, especially not if it meant Heller would go free. The bastard had to pay.

"What you got on the harvest?" Porter asked.

"The marijuana is almost fully mature. The Seekers are talking about harvesting next week, or maybe later."

"Or maybe? What the hell is that? I need the exact date!"

"Understood, but Sol hasn't set a date. Right now, he's saying the plants aren't ready."

"Jesus, we're running out of fucking time."

"I realize that." Jason noticed a group of Seekers come out of the store. "I've gotta go. I'll be in touch."

He hung up on Porter's cursing and slid the burner back into his pocket as someone started shouting angrily on the other side of the parking lot. Derrick Hanks had followed the Seekers out of the store, a six pack of beer cans in each hand.

"You motherfuckering hippie marijuana lovers had better fucking move your shit off the mountains and get the hell out of *my* forest," Hanks ranted at two young women and three men who were ignoring him, which infuriated the old logger even more.

Jason crossed the parking lot just in time to hear one of the guys say something to Hanks.

"The forest belongs to all of us, dude. It's public land. Don't let all that anger destroy your karma. Peace, love, and understanding." It was Fox.

"I'll give you a piece of my karma." Hanks's already red face turned almost purple and his knuckles whitened, his meaty fists tightening their grip on the six packs.

"Dude, you look like you could use a hit of the good stuff. It'll make you feel so much better." Fox swept his long blond hair back from his face in a practiced gesture.

His smooth words parroted the Seekers' beliefs, but Jason could tell that he was baiting the old guy and that at any moment, Hanks was going to drop the beer and the situation would turn violent. Jason stepped up to one of the Seekers and her shopping cart laden with supplies.

"Can I borrow that?" he pointed at the cart.

"Sure, Shadow," Rabbit whispered, but she nervously kept her eyes on the interchange between Hanks and Fox.

Jason took hold of the cart with both hands and shoved it between Hanks and Fox.

"What the fuck?" Hanks yelled at him.

Jason didn't reply, but when Hanks tried to lunge around him toward Fox, Jason blocked him with the cart again.

"You think you can stop me with that goddamned cart? Why don't you step away from it and fight like a man." Hanks dropped the six packs and freed his hands.

Just then, the Seekers' dented and dusty 14-passenger van, painted in wild rainbow colors, roared into the parking lot, belching clouds of exhaust. It was followed by a spotless black Hummer.

Of course he drives a fully tricked-out Hummer, Jason thought. The obnoxious vehicle boasted power, brute force, and a hefty price tag. Only a drug dealer like Rob Heller could afford a vehicle like that in rural Humboldt County.

Two long-haired, bearded Seekers climbed out of the van, and Heller got out of the Hummer. Unlike the other men, Heller was clean-shaven and sported a bald head. He wore immaculately clean clothes and carried himself light on his feet, despite the mountain of muscles rising underneath his polo shirt. There was something aggressive and challenging in how he moved, like a boxer ready for a fight.

Jason turned away from Heller and fought against the surge of hatred that made him grip the handle of the shopping cart in a stranglehold.

Gone was the poor, scrawny runt he'd known in high school, replaced by a drug kingpin and sexual predator. Not only did Heller control the transport of drugs through the Humboldt County corridor, he was also the bastard who'd hooked Jason's sister on drugs, sexually abused her, and as far as Jason was concerned, killed her. Now Heller had his eyes on Clarity.

No way, Jason scowled. It was time Heller paid for his crimes.

"What's going on here?" Heller demanded, his eyes hidden behind designer sunglasses, his perfect, white teeth gleaming bright in his tan face.

Hanks turned from Jason and the Seekers to confront this new source of irritation, his own face a mess of wild, graying beard and stained, broken teeth, his plaid shirt and jeans frayed and faded with age.

"None of your fucking business, Heller," he growled.

Heller cracked his knuckles. "Take your beer and go home, old man. You don't want to mess with me."

Everything about Heller's stance challenged Hanks, who glared back at the muscle-bound, younger man for a long, charged moment. But then his watery blue eyes wavered and shifted away. He spat at Heller's feet.

"Goddamn druggies," Hanks cursed under his breath and stomped off to his pickup.

The Seekers started wheeling their shopping carts to the van. Jason followed with his.

"Hey, where's Clarity?" Heller called out, approaching Jason.

"She didn't come shopping this time, dude." Jason continued to push the cart to the waiting van.

Heller grabbed him by the shoulder. "Why not? Doesn't she always?"

Jason grit his teeth and fought to stay calm. It took all he had not to punch Heller in the face.

"I guess she didn't feel like it," Jason shrugged against the weight of Heller's hand. No way was he going to give up information on Clarity to Heller.

Fox sauntered over. "Shadow, dude, get that shit to the van." He spoke to Jason but looked at Heller, his face carefully blank, as if he didn't know the drug dealer.

"I gotta go," Jason said.

He looked down at Heller's hand still on his shoulder, but Heller kept it there. He got the feeling that behind those dark, designer glasses Heller was studying him and assessing his unkempt hair, scraggly beard and dirty clothes. Heller's thin lips tightened and something seemed to click. He released Jason's shoulder.

"Jason Parrish. It's been a long time."

"Dude, I'm Shadow now." Jason bared his teeth in what he hoped looked like a friendly grin, fighting to maintain his laid-back, Seeker persona.

"You moved down to the City after high school, didn't you, Parrish." It wasn't a question. "You were a cop or something."

"That kind of life wasn't for me, bro." Jason shrugged again, as if he hadn't a care in the world. "Chasing money and all that stuff just doesn't measure up to life in nature. I've found peace with the Seekers. Sol has inspired me to find my inner calm. It's a beautiful thing. You should try it."

"That shit's retarded," Heller said dismissively as he flexed, his muscles bulging and rippling beneath the thin layer of his polo shirt. He turned to leave, and then added, "Too bad about your sister. She was a lot of laughs."

Jason clenched the cart handle in a death grip as he fought the urge to bash in Heller's shiny, bald head.

"See ya 'round," Jason called after Heller.

He spoke the words casually, but they were a promise. Heller was going to pay for destroying Tammy, and Jason was going to make damn sure he never hurt another woman again.

#

5:30 p.m. Friday, Humboldt County

Zoe checked the map on her phone as she approached the exit off the Redwood Highway, a four-lane road almost completely devoid of cars. A while back, she'd passed signs to the larger town of Garberville and more recently, a sign to the smaller town of Redway, but now, she saw no sign for Woodsville. According to Shadow's directions, this was her exit, but something about it didn't feel right. Maybe it was how the turnoff disappeared into the dark wall of trees that loomed up on all sides of the empty highway. If Clare didn't need her help, she'd turn tail and drive straight back to San Francisco.

From the moment she'd driven out of Sonoma's rolling wine country and into the mountainous terrain of Mendocino County, Zoe had started feeling trapped. The Arizona desert landscape she was used to spread out like an open book, filled with light and distance, the plants secondary to the physical contours of the land. Now, as she ventured further north beyond Mendocino and into rugged Humboldt County, the land grew even more wild. Here, trees towered everywhere, enormous, mysterious, and dark.

Her uneasiness grew as a white pickup truck came out of nowhere and followed her off the Redwood Highway and onto the frontage road. She switched off the car stereo so she could think, but in the silence she felt her heart beating a little too fast.

Earlier, when she was grabbing a few items for the trip, one of her roommates had told her she was crazy to go alone to Humboldt County, mentioning something about a scary movie called *Deliverance*. Zoe didn't have a choice about going alone. That roommate worked nights and her other roommate was out of town on business. She'd been too busy in the six months since moving and starting her new job to make any close, personal friends who could go with her.

She checked the rearview mirror again. In the long shadows cast by the trees, she wasn't able to get a clear view of the driver, but she could see that he was big and had a lot of wild hair on his head and face. Maybe he was simply heading to Woodsville like she was...but maybe he wasn't.

She grabbed her purse, pulled it onto her lap, and felt the reassuring heft of her gun inside. Her dad had been a cop. He'd bought her the handgun when she turned eighteen, telling her that it made him feel better about her going off alone to college. In those few months before her parents died in a car crash, she used to go with him every weekend to the shooting range for target practice. If that man behind her tried anything, he'd get one hell of a surprise.

But why stick around? She floored the gas of her little sedan and the car leapt forward. She couldn't see if the guy stayed on her tail because it took all her attention to steer around the wild twists and turns. A mile later, a sign announced Woodsville, population 300, elevation 1,010. It wasn't much of a place, but anything was better than being alone on that desolate road with that truck.

She slowed as the road morphed into a tiny main street. On one side of the street stood an all-in-one grocery and liquor store with several gas pumps out front. Across the street was a small café and several gift shops that probably catered to the tourists heading for Humboldt State Redwood Park in the summer, but now that it was late September, they were all closed.

A little farther down the street, several pickups were parked outside a storefront. A red and yellow neon sign flashed "Beer" in the long shadows cast by the tall trees in the late afternoon light. As she drove by the bar and headed out of town, she glanced in the rearview mirror and noticed the white pickup pull in beside the other trucks. She exhaled and felt some of the tension drain out of her. The guy hadn't been following her. It was Friday after five, and he'd been on his way to join his buddies at the local watering hole.

She checked Shadow's directions and her odometer again. She passed a mile marker, then a second. A bunch of little dirt roads branched off into the forest. Finally, at 2.8 miles outside of Woodsville, she spotted the dirt road Shadow had described. She took the turn and darkness closed in. She turned on her headlights and looked at the dashboard clock, surprised it wasn't yet 6 o'clock. If there weren't so many darned trees, there'd have been plenty of light. Just yesterday, she'd gone running on Baker Beach in San Francisco and watched sunset at 7 p.m.

As she left the paved road and any semblance of civilization, she wondered again about Shadow and if she'd made the right decision to trust him. She squelched her unease. If Clare was in trouble, she had to help.

She switched the car stereo back on and ignored the urge to keep checking the rearview mirror. She turned her attention back to the steep and deeply rutted road.

Definitely not a good place to bottom out, but she drove as fast as she could. The sooner she found Clare, the sooner they could both get out of there.

When Clare had told her she was leaving San Francisco to move to the Seekers' commune in the Humboldt redwoods, Zoe argued long and hard that what Clare really needed was to see a doctor and not run off chasing a magical marijuana cure to her kidney disease. The whole thing was such a bad idea, but Clare wouldn't listen to reason. Now that Zoe was here, seeing firsthand how wild and remote the Humboldt forest was, she realized that if Clare really was in trouble, then she'd done the right thing to come.

She came to a fork in the dirt road. She stopped, turned on the overhead light, and checked the directions again. Nowhere did it mention this fork. She reached for her phone. No reception. Shadow had warned her phones were useless out here.

"Now what?" she said aloud.

Maybe Shadow had forgotten this junction, damn him.

She studied each fork to see if one looked more traveled, but it was hard to tell in the glare of the headlights. For a moment, she considered going back to a place she could get cell reception, but it was going to be dark soon, and she really wanted to find Clare before then.

What the hell, she thought, and took the left fork.

She gunned the engine up the steep incline. The car stereo finished its track. She didn't bother selecting another. Her attention was fully focused on the road, which began to deteriorate with clumps of vegetation rising up from the center rut. The road shot upward and she downshifted, crawling forward in first gear.

Around the next turn, she braked to avoid a large pile of rocks that had fallen across the road and completely blocked it.

Damn, the other fork must be the right one, she thought, but there were no turnaround spots on the narrow road. There was nothing to do but back her car down the hill.

She twisted around in her seat, braced her right arm against the passenger headrest, and navigated slowly and awkwardly backwards. The steep descent, poorly illuminated by her taillights, made seeing difficult, and she cringed as a big branch screeched along the passenger side when she steered a little too far to the right. She heaved a sigh of relief when she reached the intersection and unkinked her neck.

The clock on her dash glowed 6:30 p.m. She'd been driving for more than five hours, minus a few pit stops. She stretched, arching her back, and rubbed her eyes. They felt gritty from the long drive. The last time she'd driven so far had been when she'd driven from Phoenix to San Francisco.

Maybe this fork was the right one to Harmony and Clare was just minutes away. If so, there was still time to make it back to the motel room in Garberville that she'd reserved for the night.

Zoe started up the road, which climbed steeply and was just as rutted and narrow as the first one. Just when she was about to give up hope, the road flattened and widened out.

Okay, maybe this is it, she thought and started to breathe a little easier.

She drove into a large clearing and came to another fork.

"You've got to be kidding me!" she exclaimed, stopping the car.

She looked around the large clearing. Unlike the dark forest she'd been driving through, the clearing glowed in the light of the setting sun. It had been logged and only small bushes grew up among the tree stumps. As she looked around, she realized she must have been driving on a network of old logging roads.

Shadow might have overlooked one fork in his directions, but she doubted he would have forgotten two. She looked at the clock again and sighed. It was now almost 7 p.m. There was nothing to do but turn back.

By the time she reached Woodsville, night had fallen. She had reception, so she tried calling Shadow, but he didn't pick up. She left him a pithy message, and another equally terse text, and then cruised Woodsville's main street, scanning the all-in-one liquor and convenience store in the hopes that maybe the counterperson there could help, but except for the fluorescent lights over the gas pumps, the store's lights were out. Friday nights in the boonies were dead.

She spotted one other light shining farther down the street, the neon beer sign hanging outside the bar. The trucks and a few cars were parked out front. She pulled in alongside a huge black Hummer. Trepidation fluttered through her. She'd seen enough horror movies to know that hick bars in the middle of nowhere weren't the best places for single women to venture, especially alone at night. She had no choice. She'd come all this way, and she needed help to find Clare.

***

CHAPTER TWO

7:15 p.m. Friday, Woodsville

Zoe turned off the car, opened her purse, and pulled out her gun. She held it for a moment, aware of its cold, smooth steel, its reassuring promise of firepower. No way was she going into that bar unarmed. Following the procedure her dad had drilled into her, she checked the magazine, made sure the gun's safety lock was on, and slid it back into her purse. Grabbing her leather jacket, she swung open the car door and got out.

The night was cold, but not crisp and dry like desert nights or moistly cool like San Francisco. It smelled of earth and trees. She looked up. Far above the inky black points of the treetops, myriad stars glittered, lighting the sky. In the six months since moving to San Francisco, this was the first time she'd seen any stars.

She squinted against the bright glow of the red and yellow neon beer sign to read the name of the bar, Logjammers, which was carved into an enormous, single plank of wood nailed above the door. Music thumped as she pulled open the sturdy door and stepped inside. Light, sound, and warmth flooded her senses, making her feel like a deer caught in headlights.

"Get a load of that, Jack." An enormous, older man swiveled on his barstool to check her out. He nudged his neighbor with a burly shoulder. Both men had full gray beards and wild hair.

"Hey Gorgeous, you wanna sit with us? I'll buy you a beer," the man called out to her.

"No thanks." She made eye contact with both men to show she wasn't scared of them.

She took a seat at the table closest to the door, and following her dad's advice to never turn her back on a potential threat, sat facing the men. She kept her purse on her lap for quick and easy access and pulled open the worn, laminated menu from between the salt and pepper shakers. She held it up like a shield as she covertly studied the place.

Like old time saloons, Logjammers had a wall of hard liquor bottles lined up behind the bar. An assortment of tables and chairs stood about the room, and along one wall, a jukebox pounded out '60s rock music, Led Zeppelin screaming a "Whole Lotta Love." A white-haired, bearded man stood behind the bar, which was made from a massive, split redwood log. He was serving the old boozers.

Two much younger men sat at a table toward the rear of the place. Like the others, they eyed her with interest. One had long blond hair that he kept flipping back in an affected fashion, whereas the other had absolutely no hair, neither on his clean-shaven face nor on his bald head. The bald man also wasn't wearing plaid flannel or work boots like the others but a fleece jacket and running shoes. The harsh lines of his face and the rigid way he sat as he watched her made Zoe distinctly uncomfortable. She looked down at her menu.

The old bartender came over, wiping his damp, weathered hands on his stained white apron. "Can I get you something?"

"A roast beef sandwich and coffee to go, please." She raised her voice over the blasting rock music.

"Sure thing, miss." The man nodded, his clear blue eyes assessing her before he turned away.

Zoe checked her phone, but there was still nothing from Shadow. She needed to use the bathroom, but to do so, she'd have to walk past all those ogling men. She wasn't going to let them intimidate her. She shoved her chair back, stood up, and squared her shoulders. Holding her head high, she headed for the restrooms at the back of the bar. She ignored the men as she passed them.

The women's restroom was the first door down the dark hallway. Once inside, she slid the hefty bolt into place with satisfying force. Again, she checked her phone, but there was still nothing from Shadow.

Damn it, she cursed silently. She hated feeling helpless.

She sent him yet another text and once more tried calling him, but no luck. Discouragement swept through her as she realized that he must be at Harmony where there was no reception.

She looked in the grimy mirror over the equally dirty sink. Her eyes were red and her mascara had smudged after the long hours of driving and staring at the road. She ran a hand over her hair to smooth it down and weighed her options. She could give up trying to find Clare tonight and head back to Garberville, or she could suck it up and ask one of the men in the bar for help.

#

Darkness had snuffed out any trace of daylight by the time Jason pulled into Woodsville. The timing of Fox's meeting with Heller sucked, but with his boss riding his ass for results, Jason had to work with it. He needed to learn Heller's game plan for the marijuana harvest.

Heller hadn't risen to power by being stupid. He posed as a law-abiding local organic farmer and pretended to keep his hands clean. Fox was his contact inside the Seekers, Jason would bet on it, but he needed solid proof.

Jason drove slowly by Logjammers, the only bar for miles, and cased the vehicles parked out front. Two immediately caught his eye. A small silver import was tucked in beside a black Hummer, both of which looked out of place next to the battered pickup trucks and beater cars. One of the beaters was Fox's old Subaru. Jason double-checked the license plate on the Hummer and confirmed it was Heller's. Maybe the little sedan belonged to a wayward tourist or something.

He pulled to the far end of the strip and parked. A single streetlight winked on and dimly lit the area. He got out of the truck and quietly closed the door, not bothering to lock it. He headed around to the small alleyway between the bar and the realty next door, sidestepping the dumpster and several garbage cans in the dark as he headed for Logjammer's rear service entrance.

He pushed open the door into the bright kitchen. Warm, savory air poured over him. A deep-fat fryer sizzled with an order of fries and a half-constructed sandwich lay on the counter, along with open jars of mayonnaise and mustard.

He didn't want Charlie to see him, not that the old man would recognize him in this getup, but he didn't want to lie to his dad's old friend about what he was doing there. He avoided the swinging doors that led into the main barroom and swiftly crossed the kitchen to the side hallway, which lay in shadows under a burned-out light bulb.

He cracked open the first door at the back of the hallway and peeked inside. His memory hadn't failed him. It was still a utility closet, as it had been when he worked as a busboy in high school. Next door was the men's room. He sidled past it and the women's room, his back flattened against the wall so he could observe the main barroom.

At the table nearest him, two men sat together. He recognized Heller's smooth bald head and Fox's long blond hair and ratty coat. He strained to hear what they were saying, but it was impossible over the jukebox and the guys carousing at the bar. He watched Fox set down a foaming pint of beer and wipe his beard on the back of his sleeve.

Just then, the toilet flushed behind him in the women's restroom. He slipped down the hall and into the utility closet.

#

Zoe swung open the bathroom door, intending to make a beeline for her table past the gauntlet of men. Instead, she collided with the dangerous-looking bald man. She jumped back.

"Excuse me," she said loudly over Mick Jagger's blaring voice and the Rolling Stones.

The man braced his hand on the hallway wall, blocking her path. Her heart started to race. She tried to sidestep him, but he shifted his stance and raised his other arm, planting a hand on the opposite wall of the narrow hallway. He smelled of expensive cologne and musky male, and he was standing way too close. She almost took a step back, but then she got mad. The guy was being a jerk.

"I said, 'Excuse me.'" She looked pointedly at the arm barring her way and then up into his small, black eyes, his clean-shaven face an expressionless mask. She had the unpleasant feeling he was enjoying her discomfort. The Stones' song ended and the jukebox went silent.

"Where you from, babe?" He looked at her hair.

Maybe he was hitting on her, but there was something off about him. No way was she going to ask him for help finding Clare. She wanted to get away from him as fast as possible.

"The big city. Now, if you don't mind—" She pointed past him to the bright barroom.

"Where you headed?" His eyes crawled slowly over her.

"I'm on my way to visit my sister. Now, let me by."

She lunged sideways, trying to angle around him, but he anticipated the move. He grabbed her by the upper arms.

"Let go of me!" She jerked her arms backwards, trying to break free of his iron-strong grip.

"You got fire," he grinned, his mouth filled with too perfect, bleached-white teeth. "Must be that hair."

He let her arms go and reached up with one hand to stroke her hair. She slapped him away.

"Don't touch me!" She gripped her purse, feeling for her gun.

"Hey, Heller, you comin'?" A voice behind the man called.

"Too bad I can't stick around to get better acquainted." He looked her over one last, long time, his eyes flat and emotionless, like the gaze of a wild predator. "I'll be seeing you around, Red."

Not if I can help it, she thought as the creepy guy turned away and another Led Zeppelin tune started to pump from the jukebox.

#

Jason listened through the utility closet door to a woman being harassed by Heller. She said she was on her way to visit her sister.

Crap. Jason remembered the little silver import parked out front. The woman had to be Clarity's sister, Zoe, but what the hell was she doing here? She was supposed to have gone to Harmony.

He was undercover to bust Heller on drug charges, not police Heller's twisted sex life, but after Tammy and now Clarity, no way could he not get involved.

He tensed, ready to act. Zoe had no idea who she was dealing with. Heller was a goddamned sexual predator who'd fixated on Clarity. He hoped to God Zoe wouldn't let it slip that she was Clarity's sister, but then he realized she was smartly keeping her answers vague.

In the pause between jukebox tunes, he heard a man call for Heller. He cracked the door open and watched Zoe move away from him and into the bar.

Jason didn't need to see her face to know she was hot. He could tell by the way she moved that her trim body was in kick-ass shape. The old loggers were checking her out, but she acted like she didn't give a damn. Unlike Clarity, she wasn't timid or blond. Her dark red hair hung in waves to her shoulders. He watched her sit down and take out a phone.

Oh hell. Was she trying to reach him? He'd borrowed an old high school friend's pickup for this case, but the cigarette charger was busted. He'd been relying on a solar charger, but his phone was currently out of juice. He'd have to check in with her later. First priority was Heller, who'd just left the bar with Fox.

Jason slipped back through the kitchen and out the rear entrance, quickly retracing his steps to the mouth of the alley. Voices around the corner pulled him up short. Heller and Fox were talking, no more than five feet away.

"Did you get a load of that hair? I'd love to sample that fire pussy." Heller smacked his lips crudely.

"You buy her story that she's just 'passing through'? She could be a Fed, sniffing around."

"Let her sniff. She can sniff me anytime, the bitch," Heller muttered. "The fucking Feds aren't after you, Fox, and I'm just an upstanding organic farmer, right?"

Jason heard the strike of a match and cigarette smoke wafted to him on the gentle night breeze.

Heller continued, "Sol got a date for the harvest?"

"Shouldn't be more than a week's, my guess. He's watching the buds for maximum peak. Dude, they're fucking enormous already. You should see 'em."

There was a pause and more cigarette smoke headed Jason's way.

When Heller next spoke, his voice roughened. "Why didn't the girl come to Redway today? You told me she was going to be there."

"I tried, but she wouldn't."

"She 'wouldn't'? What the fuck is that? I told you to bring her."

"I tried, man—"

"You know goddamned well I can't go anywhere near the Seekers or the grow."

"Dude, I know. Like I said, I tried, but—"

"Damn it!"

Something hit the wall so hard Jason felt it vibrate against his back. It must have been Heller's fist.

"Take it easy, dude." Fox sounded nervous.

"Get me the fucking girl," Heller snarled.

"Look, I gotta get going," Fox said hastily, a car door creaking open. "Dude, you wanna see her, you better sneak up to Harmony yourself." The door slammed and Fox's ancient Subaru whined to life.

Jason gazed up at the narrow slice of sky visible between the two buildings. The distant stars twinkled, but their sparkling beauty did nothing to calm the rage boiling inside him. Heller was a sick fuck who had to be stopped. His drug running was bad enough, but this was personal. Heller had destroyed his kid sister and was now after Clarity. Poor girl. Jason hadn't known about her kidney problems, but between her health and Heller, she was in double trouble. He had to get her sister back to Harmony pronto, before Heller showed up there.

The moment the Hummer's overbuilt engine roared into the night, Jason headed around the corner to the Logjammer's front entrance.

#

The jukebox shut off, leaving the bar for a moment in echoing silence. A plate clattered in the kitchen.

What's taking the bartender so long? Zoe thought with irritation.

She should've asked him right away about getting to Harmony, but chances were, none of these men had ever heard of Harmony and she was just wasting precious time.

She looked at the men sitting at the bar. They didn't seem to realize the music had ended and were still speaking loudly.

"God damn Heller, that fucking drug dealer!" The biggest, burliest man slammed a fist onto the redwood bar top. "Him and all those tree-hugging hippies and environmentalists, they all fucked us. Remember how it used to be?"

"Come on, Derrick, those days ain't coming back," said the man on the barstool next to him.

"A man could earn a decent living around here logging the trees." Derrick kept talking, waving a hand in the air for emphasis. "My pop and his pop, they bought land and built their own homes, all on *honest* hard work. They were able to make enough money to give their wives and kids, *their families*, a decent way of life. I'm so goddamn sick of making peanuts and living in that shithole trailer." He tossed back a shot of the liquor and wiped his grizzled beard with the back of his hand.

"We just need a couple more of them big trees and we'll be golden, right?" said his buddy. "Couple hundred grand, then we can pay off the rig and the dozer."

"Heller's half our age and rolling in cash." Derrick drained the last few drips of the liquor bottle into his shot glass. "He didn't have to work for it, not like us, slaving our asses off for what, huh? Diddly-squat? Jesus, there's so much goddamned money in drugs. You know, I think maybe we're in the wrong goddamn business." He tossed back the last of his drink, belched loudly, and then swiveled on his barstool and bellowed toward the kitchen, "Charlie! I need another!"

He noticed Zoe and leered at her. "Hey Gorgeous, you don't have to sit there all by your lonesome. Why don't you come join us? We can show you a good time."

"Yeah, a real good time," his buddy chuckled and waggled his eyebrow at her.

I'll show them exactly why I won't give them a good time, she scowled, but then the bartender hurried out of the kitchen carrying a paper cup and a bag.

"Be right there, Derrick. Just hold your horses on that next round," he said to the big man and his friend as he bustled by them.

"Sorry for the delay, miss. Here's your order." He put the items on the table.

"Thanks," she said. "Maybe you can help me? I'm looking for a place called Harmony. You heard of it?"

Charlie squinted at her, his blue eyes surprisingly astute under tufted white eyebrows. "Sure, but what does a good girl like you wanna do with them bunch of weirdoes?"

"My sister's with them. She's sick and needs my help." Zoe pushed back her chair, stood up, and pulled her wallet from her purse. "You know how to get there?"

"Sorry about your sister, miss." The bartender took her cash. "Harmony's up one of them logging roads not far outside of town, but it's a good ways out in the forest. Hey Derrick," he called to the men at the bar. "You guys know how to get to where them Seekers are hanging out?"

Derrick lurched off his stool and lumbered over. "Hell yeah, I do. Them fucking potheads are squatting on *our* land and mooching *our* water to grow *their* weed." Fumes of alcohol rose off him in waves.

"Now, Derrick, you know that's public land you're talking about. It's National Forest."

"Fuck, you know what I mean. Get me another goddamned whiskey! I'm thirsty."

The bartender turned to Zoe. "Sorry I can't help you," he said and then gave Derrick a warning look before heading back to the bar to pour another round for the men.

Derrick looked at Zoe. "What you want with them potheads? You could have a much better time with us, sugar."

"Thanks, but no thanks," she said. Even if these men knew the way to Harmony, their hatred of the Seekers meant she couldn't trust any directions they might offer.

Garberville, here I come, she thought with resignation and grabbed the to-go bag and the cup of coffee.

Zoe shouldered her way out of the bar and smacked blindly into someone big. Hard hands gripped her shoulders. She could see nothing in the darkness after the bright lights of the bar. Had that horrible bald-headed guy waited outside for her? Fear gave way to rage.

"Let me go!" she shouted. She threw down the coffee and the bag and rammed her knee viciously upward, trying to smash the guy in the groin.

"I don't think so." The man moved deftly aside, his hands still on her shoulders.

"I said, 'Let go of me!'" she screamed and swung a booted kick at the man's shin.

The barroom doors burst open and light poured out into the dark night. She saw the man she was struggling with. He definitely wasn't bald or beardless, but very hairy and smelled pungently of wood smoke and patchouli.

"Take your filthy hands off the little lady," Derrick yelled, lunging out of the bar, his burly buddy close behind.

"Hey now, friends." The man released his grip on Zoe's shoulders and she sprang out of the way as he held his hands up in a gesture of surrender. "No need for trouble here. The lady and I have some business together. Why don't you go back inside and have another round?"

"I ain't your friend, you fucking tree-hugging environmentalist freak!" Derrick threw a violent punch at the man, but it never connected.

The man feinted to the side and then spun a lightning kick at Derrick's chest. It knocked the bigger man flat to the ground.

Derrick's buddy yelled angrily and rushed the man, who moved so fast that Zoe only saw a whirling blur of shadows and heard the dull thuds of impact and the oomphs of exhaled breath. Seconds later, Derrick's buddy also lay at his feet.

"They were just trying to defend me!" she shouted, shocked by the violence.

"Hey, what're you mad at me for? They attacked me first!"

"If you hadn't grabbed me, they wouldn't have had to." She looked down at the men lying on the ground. "Are they going to be OK?"

"Sure." His voice dropped. "You're Zoe Thompson, right?"

"Yes?"

"I'm Shadow. I called you about Clarity this morning."

"Her name is Clare, I told you that," she said, irritated at having to repeat herself.

"Whatever. Why aren't you at Harmony?"

"Because your directions sucked."

One of the men on the pavement groaned loudly and started to sit up.

"Let's get out of here." Shadow started toward the cars.

"Just a minute." Zoe's brain raced with questions. "You need to explain a few things to me before I go anywhere with you, like what the hell are you doing here? Why aren't you with Clare?"

Shadow jingled a set of keys impatiently in his pocket and looked at her for a moment. "I came looking for you. Now, let's go."

"How did you know it was me coming out of the bar?" She didn't move.

"Right," Shadow muttered, the word coming out like an expletive. "Logjammers is the only place around these parts that's open this time of night, and that," he gestured at her car, which looked positively dainty next to the monster trucks beside it, "is a dead giveaway. Satisfied?"

"I guess."

She tried to make out his features in the dim lighting outside the bar, but all she could really see was that he was big, tall, and hairy like the older guys he'd fought, but without their massive bulk.

"Come on!" Shadow turned away.

Zoe unlocked her car and watched him climb into one of the pickups, wondering if she was about to make a huge mistake. All she knew about this man called Shadow was that he claimed to know where her sister was and that he was a peace-loving member of the Seekers. But if that was true, then how come he fought better than anyone she'd ever seen?

***

CHAPTER THREE

8 p.m. Friday, Woodsville

Jason waited for Zoe to start her car. He rubbed his shin and cursed under his breath. His leg was still throbbing with pain where she'd kicked him. To be fair, she hadn't known who he was, but it pissed him off that he hadn't seen it coming.

He shoved the truck into gear and pulled away from Logjammers, Zoe on his tail. They drove out of Woodsville and into the forest. Beyond the narrow beams of their headlights, darkness enveloped the two cars.

Clarity had told him she was terrified of how dark it was in the redwood forest at night. The trees loomed so tall they blocked out the night sky overhead. She'd said that night in the forest was nothing like night in the desert where she was from. He wondered what Zoe thought of the redwood forest. He doubted she was scared.

He spotted the tiny dirt road leading to Harmony. He turned on his indicator and checked his rearview mirror to make sure Zoe stayed with him.

The truck bucked over a large rock and Jason gripped the wheel with both hands to keep the tires from jerking sideways. He downshifted to first gear and gunned the engine up the steep, rocky dirt road.

No question about it, Sol had picked about as remote a location as he could for his commune.

That's precisely the problem, Jason frowned. *They were sitting ducks.*

The very distance from civilization and its laws made the commune hopelessly vulnerable, not only to the elements and the animals that prowled the forest, but also to predator outlaws like Heller.

He thought about what he'd learned from eavesdropping on Heller and Fox outside Logjammers. As he'd hoped, he'd verified Fox was Heller's contact inside the Seekers. More disturbing, however, was discovering how much of an obsession Heller had developed for Clarity.

He scowled in the dark cab of the truck.

Clarity and Zoe weren't his problem, at least they shouldn't be. He was working undercover to bring down Heller on drug charges. Still, he couldn't just stand by and ignore Clarity's plight, not after what had happened to his own sister. He'd help keep Clarity safe, at least until Zoe got her away from Harmony. If anyone could persuade Clarity to leave Sol, he suspected Zoe was it. He hadn't known her long, but he got the sense that she was a force to be reckoned with.

A half hour later, Jason cornered around a big tree and the truck's headlights lit up the plywood arch announcing their arrival at Harmony. He drove under it and down a short stretch to a parking area where an old rusted van and a dirt bike were parked. Fox's ancient Subaru was also there. Zoe pulled up beside him, her unblemished little silver import as alien as she seemed in this wild land.

#

Zoe switched off her car. The abrupt shift from bright headlights to black night blinded her and she rubbed her eyes. The road to Harmony had seemed endless, bumpy rocks and twisty, mountainous climbs, walled in by giant trees, until she'd finally followed Shadow's truck under a sign announcing their arrival at the commune.

Perhaps "sign" was too fancy a word for the big piece of plywood mounted to two redwood trees on either side of the road. Someone had painted the colors of the rainbow across the panel and scrawled 'HARMONY' in white across it, but the paint had run so much that the word was a barely legible blur.

She grabbed her purse, feeling the bulky shape of her handgun through the leather as she climbed out of the car. Before shutting off her headlights, all she'd seen had been that lousy sign and a few cars parked in a clearing in the forest. As far as she could tell, she and Shadow were in the middle of nowhere, completely alone.

"Ready?" Shadow's deep voice came to her through the dark silence.

"Yes," she said. She just wanted to find Clare and get the hell out of there.

Shadow started to move away in the dark.

"How can you see where you're going?" she asked after a couple of faltering steps. She could barely make him out against the black background of the trees.

"I know the way. Take my hand," he said.

"I'm OK," she said, but then tripped over a root.

"Don't be stubborn."

She scowled but took his hand. It was big, warm, and reassuring.

Reassuring? She scowled again. She didn't need reassurance.

Her eyes began to adapt as Shadow led her along a footpath. She sensed, more than saw, the massive girth of trees rising up on each side of the narrow trail. They had to be old-growth redwoods, they were so big. She'd seen photographs of old-growth redwoods, but they did no justice to the trees' prehistorically gargantuan size. She felt tiny.

The chilly night smelled damp, not salty damp like San Francisco. It smelled somehow greener. She'd never smelled moss before, but this had to be what it smelled like. The soft tread of their footsteps made almost no sound on the spongy ground.

Can you hear silence? she wondered.

Night for her had always been inhabited by ambient sounds. San Francisco and Phoenix had city sounds, mainly traffic or the occasional siren, and even in the desert, there was always a night wind blowing, or the distant roar of a plane overhead. But here, there was nothing. Her ears rang with it.

"How far do we have to go?" she asked after a few hundred feet or so, her voice sounding muffled in the eerie silence.

"Not much farther. Careful here." Shadow's voice came low and intimate in the dark, his grip tightening on hers as they crossed a small depression strewn with a few rocks.

The wall of trees abruptly stopped and a clearing opened up. From what she could make out, Harmony wasn't much more than a motley collection of tents, a fire ring, and several wooden picnic tables. A fire crackled brightly in the fire ring, surrounded by people bundled in blankets and thick coats. They were talking quietly, their faces flickering in the firelight.

Zoe shook off Shadow's hand and eagerly scanned the group for Clare, but her sister wasn't there. A tall man with white, shoulder-length hair and a long, flowing beard stood up as they approached the group by the fire. He looked about seventy, Zoe guessed, but who knew what lay behind all that white hair?

"Good evening, Solace. This is Zoe Thompson, Clarity's sister." Shadow addressed the older man with respect.

"We are so glad you have come." The older man held out his hand to her and his mouth creased in a paternal smile. "'Solace' is much too formal. Please call me 'Sol.'"

Zoe glared at the man, who her sister had met at a pot club in San Francisco. Clare claimed he'd inspired her move to Humboldt.

More like lured her, Zoe thought sourly.

According to Clare, Sol held secret knowledge that would cure her kidney problems. He had a lot to answer for.

Zoe clenched her teeth. It had been a long trip, a very long trip, and part of her wanted to cut the crap and demand: "Where's Clare?" But she knew that sometimes you just had to stuff it all down and paste on a smile to get what you wanted. She peeled back her lips and held out a hand to the Seeker leader.

"Hello, Sol," she said with a smile.

The secure grip of his handshake surprised her. She'd assumed he was old and frail, but there was none of that in the hand that shook hers. It pulsed with strength and an electric vitality, warm against her cold skin. She let out a long breath, then as calmly as she could, asked the question she was burning to know.

"So, Sol, where is my sister?"

#

Jason watched Zoe encounter Sol with amusement. They were diametrically opposed personality types, the one task-oriented and practical, the other focused almost entirely on the spiritual.

Sol held Zoe's hand and stared intently at her in the flickering firelight with his wide blue eyes.

"It is such a pleasure to meet you, Zoe. Clarity has spoken to me about you on so many occasions. You are important to her, such a loving big sister. Your actions convey your love, coming all this way to see her." He didn't let go of Zoe's hand right away.

"Thanks, I guess." She gave him a forced smile and then shook her hand free of his. "Where's Clare?"

Jason found himself impressed by Zoe's ability to stand up to Sol, who tended to manipulate people by flattering them with compliments or mesmerizing them with truisms so that he usually got his own way.

Sol stroked his long beard as he studied Zoe, nodding to himself, as if he'd decided something about her. He waved toward one of the tents. "She is over there."

"Thanks," Zoe said and rushed off.

Jason went with Sol to the people gathered around the fire. About half the Seekers were there, a ragtag mix of mostly well-intentioned but misguided young men and women. In the month he'd joined them, Jason had seen their numbers swell to more than thirty members, mostly young people looking for community and hoping to work the high grade marijuana grows and be paid in cash or kind. Nicknamed "trimmigrants," they came to help harvest and trim the marijuana in preparation for export and to be welcomed into Sol's commune. He'd used the same story when he'd joined the Seekers.

The air around the campfire was thick with wood smoke and the pungent scent of marijuana. Jason crouched down beside a guy who was sitting on the ground, holding a large, intricately blown glass bong.

"Hey Shadow, you wanna hit?" The guy's voice was ragged as clouds of pot smoke streamed from his mouth.

"Thanks, dude, not right now. My hands are too cold."

Jason held his hands to the warming blaze, knowing the excuse was lame, but no one else seemed to notice as the bong bypassed him. He'd never do drugs if he could possibly avoid it, not so much because of his job but because he wanted to honor Tammy's memory.

Sol addressed the group, though his eyes followed the wood smoke, wandering upward into the night sky. "Practice patience with Clarity's sister, my friends. She has not yet seen the truth and the light, but she will. She is a fiery soul, a maker of her own destiny. She is truly a daughter of Pele. Do you all know Pele? She is the Hawaiian goddess of fire and the maker of new land." He pressed his hands together, placed them against his chest, and bowed his head as if in prayer.

"How very beautiful. 'Pele,' I love it!" Luna said, taking the bong and inhaling deeply.

Like Sol, Luna was much older than the other Seekers and had flowing gray hair. She also acted like Sol's wife, though Jason had never heard marriage mentioned. She exhaled a long, steady stream of smoke from her nostrils. A dreamy smile lit her face as she looked up at Sol.

"I just love how you can reach the inner essence and touch the true soul of everyone you meet. You have such a way with names, Sol."

"Right on," someone muttered.

Several other people around the fire nodded and bowed their heads.

"Whoa, I just realized something," a girl on the opposite side of the fire piped up. "Names are the secret to understanding life, aren't they? I mean, we can't really know the world until we can name it, right?"

Jason nodded along with the others but only half-listened to the trippy talk.

The fact that Sol renamed people with what he deemed their inner, "true" qualities was another way he built his web of influence around them. In that respect, Sol did fit the bill of a cult leader, exerting control over their identities, but despite Sol's claim to inner spiritual insight, the man seemed pretty clueless about how real power worked, the kind that forced submission, the kind of blunt power Heller wielded. Even so, Jason kept thinking about Sol's name for Zoe. "Pele, the goddess of fire"—it fit her perfectly.

#

Zoe pulled back the door flap of the big, old-fashioned, canvas tent. She looked inside but couldn't see anything in the dark. She heard the rustle of blankets.

"Clare, are you in there?"

"Zoe?"

Relieved to hear her sister's voice, Zoe slipped into the tent. After being outside, the tent felt warm and humid and smelled thickly of sandalwood incense. A match sparked and a candle sitting on a milk crate by the door flickered to life. She could just make out her sister's pale face in the dim light. Clare was alone and huddled under a big mound of blankets that were piled everywhere on the floor. It looked like a lot of people shared the sleeping space.

"Hi, sweetie," Zoe said, moving closer.

Clare struggled to sit up. "Shadow said he was going to call you, but I was hoping you wouldn't bother to come."

"Never a bother, Sis. Sorry it's so late. It was a long trip from the City. Give me a hug." Zoe leaned over and embraced Clare, whose shoulders felt bird-bone thin through the blanket.

It was too dark with the single candle to get a good look at her sister. She spotted a box of matches and two other candles on the milk crate beside the burning candle and smoking censor. She lit the additional candles and the space brightened considerably, though her eyes watered in the blue, incense-thick smoke. As always, she was struck by Clare's beauty, her luminous blue eyes and long blond hair, but she looked beyond Clare's smile and saw the pallor, the hair that hung dirty and lank, the dullness in her eyes.

"How are you feeling?" she asked.

"I'm OK. You really didn't need to come," Clare said, shaking her head. "I'm in good hands. Sol has been a healing godsend to me. His energy is so powerful and he's so wise. He says the big trees here carry deep wisdom of ancient times, when humans lived closer to nature, more in tune with the world and the greater harmony of life. I know he's right." She pulled the blankets higher around her, her voice passionate. "There's something wonderful and magical about this place. I feel it all around me, all the time. The air is so pure. And the water! It's straight from a spring coming down from the mountain, with no chemicals or stuff in it. I feel better here, better than I have since mom and dad died."

"Great," Zoe bit out, struggling to keep her temper. Clare was in total denial! She had no idea how clichéd and ridiculous she sounded, and bringing their parents' death into it made Zoe even angrier. What about all the time she'd spent taking care of Clare, providing for her, taking her to the doctors? She'd done all she could to make sure she had a job with good enough health insurance that Clare could see the best kidney specialists in the City.

"Shadow must have had a good reason to call me," Zoe insisted. "He said something about a bad man?"

"Bad man?" Clare looked puzzled. "I don't know who he's talking about. There are no bad men here." Clare's smile faded, as if her earlier enthusiasm had taken a toll. She lay back against the pile of pillows and closed her eyes. "I have been feeling tired, but it's just the anemia. Rabbit's been giving me extra lentils. They're a great vegan source of iron, you know."

"Good, I'm glad you're trying to be proactive, but are you having any uremia, or muscle cramps, or any other symptoms that your kidney function's getting worse?"

"I'm fine." Clare kept her eyes closed.

"Anemia's one of the first signs of kidney problems." Zoe didn't want to push too hard and spook her sister, but if Clare went into kidney failure, she risked falling into a coma and dying. "Please, Sis, let's get you checked out by a"—she stopped herself from saying "real"—"doctor, OK?"

Clare opened her eyes and frowned at Zoe. "Western medicine doesn't have all the answers. It doesn't treat the whole patient. That's why I've never been healed. Sol knows things, deeper things, things that are truer than anything your "doctors" can tell me. I know it, Zoe, in my heart and in my soul, I know it. He'll cure me, you'll see." Clare's conviction was undermined by her wan skin and the shadows under her eyes.

"Maybe you're right, but why not benefit from the best of both worlds?"

"I told you, Sol's all I need. He has a background in medicine, did you know that?"

"No." Zoe had passed him off as some kind of New Age, aging hippie.

"Yes, and he almost died of cancer a few years ago, too."

Now that was surprising. Sol struck her as healthy as a horse, and he seemed extremely fit for an older man.

Clare continued, "He learned how to use cannabis for healing at a place in the City. I met him there when he came down from Humboldt to meet with the director and give a seminar about the Seekers and their mission. When I told him about my health, he encouraged me to join the Seekers. We're all seeking healing and greater harmony with the forces at work in the world and the universe."

Zoe only half-listened as she tried to figure out how to convince Clare to come with her.

"That all sounds great, Clare—"

"My name is Clarity now," her sister interjected.

"OK, Clarity, if you're feeling so great, what would it hurt for you to come with me for a day to see a doctor? Hear me out," she said when her sister rolled her eyes. "You know I want what's best for you, right? I love you! So for me, will you come and let the doctor check you out? I made an appointment for first thing tomorrow in Garberville with the nephrologist. Come with me now and you'll be back here by lunchtime tomorrow, I swear."

"I love you, too," Clare said and sighed. Zoe could tell she was capitulating. She gave Zoe a resigned look. "OK, I'll go with you, but do we have to leave this instant?"

Zoe fought to keep from rushing her. She wanted nothing more than to be safely out of the dark forest and in a motel room with electric lights, a shower, and a comfy bed.

"I'm afraid so. We're lucky the doctor's even available tomorrow, what with it being the weekend."

"OK, let me get my stuff together," Clare said, pushing the covers off.

Zoe leaned over and gave her a hug. "I'm so glad! Can I help you?"

"No thanks. I just need to get out of my PJs and pack a few things."

"Great. I'll go and let Shadow know."

Zoe climbed out of the tent, feeling relieved. The Seekers were still gathered by the fire. She looked over the collection of long-haired and bearded men and realized Shadow wasn't among them. She heard other voices by the picnic tables where a gas lantern shone brightly. Shadow sat at one of the tables eating. A petite, long-haired young woman stood beside him.

As she headed over to them, Zoe smelled something spicy and delicious on the night air. Now that everything was settled, she realized she was starving.

"Clare's going to come with me," she announced to Shadow.

"Great," Shadow said and then burst out coughing. He grabbed a ceramic mug from the table and took a big gulp. He cleared his throat. "This is Rabbit. She's the camp cook." His husky voice sounded rougher than usual and his eyes watered as he introduced the woman standing beside him.

"Would you like some soup? There's still some left." Rabbit spoke in a rushed, breathy voice, as if she were scared, her eyes darting everywhere but Zoe.

"Thanks," Zoe said, thinking "Rabbit" was the perfect name for her.

Rabbit dashed over to the other picnic table where a big pot sat atop a camp stove. Zoe's stomach rumbled so loudly Shadow heard it.

"Hungry?" he said, taking another sip from his mug.

"Yes!" she said, sitting down at the table.

It was his fault she'd dropped her sandwich and coffee outside that bar in Woodsville, but none of that mattered now. For the first time since he'd called her about Clare, she felt lighthearted, knowing Clare was going to get the help she needed.

"Sol says our bodies should not be the tombs for any creatures, so we don't eat any meat," Jason said, finishing his soup.

"I can do vegetarian," Zoe nodded. Clare had been a vegetarian since high school.

Rabbit brought over a bowl of steaming soup and a spoon. "It's curry lentil," she said in that scared voice of hers and then scampered away.

Zoe took a cautious sip of the soup, curious and a little skeptical that something prepared in such rough conditions would be any good. She was pleasantly surprised. The soup was warm, thick with lentils, and seasoned just the way she liked it, hot and spicy.

"This is delicious," she said, taking a bigger spoonful.

Shadow rotated his position and straddled the picnic bench to look at her.

"You like spicy food, huh?" he said.

"Yes and yum! You eat pretty well out here."

"Uh, yeah." He was still sipping from his mug. "You need some water?"

"Sure." She ate some more soup as he got her a mug of water.

"You don't like spicy food?" she asked, when he brought back the water.

"Not so much," he chuckled, handing her the mug.

She put it on the table and finished the soup, scraping around the bottom of the bowl for every last drop. She took a sip of water. Shadow was watching her, his eyes focused on her mouth as she licked her lips. For a moment, she wondered what he looked like under all that facial hair.

She set the mug down. "You were right to call me. Clare wouldn't have agreed to come so easily if she didn't know on some gut level that her kidney disease is acting up."

"What did you say?" His mouth kicked upward in a grin and his eyes glinted in the lantern light.

"She didn't give me any trouble—"

"No, what you said first—"

He was laughing at her!

"You heard me just fine," she snapped.

"I want to hear you say it again," he said softly, so only she could hear.

"Why?" She arched an eyebrow at him. Two could play this game.

"Come on, just say it, please?" Laughter threaded his voice.

"You mean, 'You were right?'"

"Ah, music to my ears." Now he was laughing outright. "You don't say that very often, do you?"

"I don't have to, because I usually am right." She wasn't going to give him the satisfaction of gloating, so she got up from the table. "I wonder what's taking Clare so long?"

She turned toward the tent just as the crack of a gunshot pierced the night.

***

CHAPTER FOUR

Friday night, Harmony

Pure instinct made Zoe drop to the ground. Everything had gone dark, the lantern snuffed, the fire spluttering from water someone had thrown on it. Her heart slammed in her chest and her knee hurt from where it had banged on a rock. Another gunshot ripped through the night. People were running every which way, screaming.

"Down, get down!" a guy yelled. It sounded like Shadow.

Damn it, where was her purse?

She needed her gun. She scrabbled blindly in the dirt, but then remembered she'd left her purse on the picnic table. A myriad curses skittered through her brain as she prepared to make a move for the table.

Another gunshot echoed through the trees.

Forget the gun! It was too dangerous to stand up. *What about Clare?*

The tent stood less than ten feet away, its hulking outline looming in the dark. She got onto her hands and knees and crawled as fast as she could across the distance, wincing as her bruised knee banged more rocks. Her hand brushed canvas and relief swept through her. She sat back on her haunches and ran her hands over the tent, trying to find the opening.

"Clare?" she called out as loudly as she dared.

A bullet whizzed by and cracked into a nearby tree. Had that been a stray bullet, or was a shooter targeting her? If so, she was a sitting duck.

She dropped to her belly and wriggled as fast as she could into the closest stand of trees, hoping to God her sister was somewhere safe and not in the tent. She made it behind the first tree and rolled over a pile of leaves and pine needles, but then she started to slide downwards.

Yikes! She was sliding out of control down into some kind of gully.

She kicked and clawed at the bristly redwood needles and fallen branches that scratched her face and tangled in her hair as she tried desperately to stop sliding. Finally, about twenty feet down, she managed to stop. She clung to the hillside, hugging the earth with all her might, and waited for her pulse to slow.

Ice cold water started to seep into her boots. Was there a creek or pool of water below her? When she tried to lift her feet out of the water, she began to slide again. She dug her boots back into the hillside. Who knew how deep the water was. Better wet boots than the rest of her body.

Silence descended on the night. She inhaled and held her breath, listening with all her might, trying to hear what was happening up the hill at Harmony. The hushed sound of water trickled below her, but nothing else. Her ears rang in the silence and tension screamed through her.

Had Clare gotten away? Was she safe? What about

Shadow? And who on earth was shooting at them? Whoever it was, they were armed. Just as obviously, the Seekers weren't, and now she wasn't, either.

What to do?

As the adrenaline wore off, the coldness of the earth stole into her body, and her wet feet felt like ice. She had to get moving or freeze. The attackers must have left by now, certainly the Seekers had. She needed her purse. Not only did it have her gun in it, but her cell phone, ID, and money. She had to climb back up and get it.

Sinking her fingers into the ground for traction, she slowly pulled her way up the embankment. When she reached the top, she cautiously peered into the clearing. It was lit by eerie white moonlight. Except for the ghostly curl of smoke rising from the dying fire, there was no sign of any movement. She headed for the picnic tables. She made it less than two yards when someone flew out of the darkness and threw her to the ground.

Her breath knocked out of her as she crashed face down into the musty dirt. The guy on top of her weighed a ton. She struggled violently, trying to get out from under him, but she had no leverage. A big hand wrapped over her mouth and a voice whispered, a husky breath in her ear.

"Shhh. It's me, Shadow."

She let out a whoosh of relief, but then got mad. He didn't need to knock her flat! She resisted the urge to bite his hand and wriggled sideways, trying to slide out from under him.

"Stop moving. We gotta get out of here." His whiskers tickled her cheek.

She twisted her head sideways, freeing her mouth. "I need my purse."

"No time."

As if on cue, a loud crashing sound came out of the trees.

"Heh, heh, we got those mother fuckin' hippies on the run!" A huge man stumbled out of the forest, belching and laughing loudly, followed by more men.

Shadow hauled Zoe to her feet. He grabbed her hand and tugged her after him. They sprinted for the trees opposite the embankment where she'd first fled. She tensed as they ran, expecting at any moment to feel a bullet rip into her, but they made it safely to cover. They went a short ways before Shadow stopped. She pulled her hand free of his.

"Where's Clare?" she whispered, trying to see him in the dark. His face was hidden in shadows.

"She's OK. I saw her leave with Sol." He stood motionless, listening.

Loud shouts, more laughter, and the sound of smashing glass crashed through the night.

"Where did they go?" she asked after a moment.

Shadow pulled her close, speaking fast and low. "I know you're worried about your sister, but we've got bigger problems right now. Those men are drunk and armed."

"Stop manhandling me!" She shook his hands off her shoulders and took a step back. "What the hell is going on? Who are those lunatics?"

"Does it matter? They've got guns and we don't. Let's get to the cars and get the hell out of here."

He turned away from her and started downhill through the trees. She could barely make him out against the black backdrop of the forest but he glanced back to make sure she was following him and then picked up speed. The guy must have bat vision or something, because none of the moonlight penetrated the dense forest canopy. She stumbled and caught herself against the rough bark of a tree.

Damn it! She'd lost him.

Like his name, Shadow had disappeared into the darkness. There was nothing to do but press on. As she groped blindly forward, a sinking feeling grew in the pit of her stomach. Her key was in her purse. Without it, her car was useless.

Shadow materialized out of the darkness. "We've got trouble."

This time, she didn't object when he took her hand again. He led her into the parking lot.

#

Damn, Jason cursed silently to himself.

Hanks and his buddies had done a bang-up job destroying their vehicles. His pickup had four flat tires. Zoe's little city car was even more thoroughly disabled, its tires slashed and its windshield smashed. The Seekers' van was only marginally in better shape, but he didn't have the key to it.

"My car!" Zoe yanked her hand free of his and lunged toward her wrecked car.

Jason let her go. He'd already checked to make sure the coast was clear, at least for now.

"What kind of assholes would do this?" She turned to him, her face in the bright moonlight full of outraged disbelief.

"Drunken, angry, and desperate men. Remember that guy at the bar, Derrick Hanks?" He pointed to the two monster pick ups parked at the far end of the parking area.

"I thought I recognized his voice."

"He wants to run the Seekers out of the forest, from what I can tell."

"Why?"

"It's complicated. I'll explain later, but we'd better get going before he and his buddies come back."

"Where?"

"Looks like we're spending the night in the woods."

"No way! Where's Clare?" She faced him, her hands on her hips. Her curly dark hair bounced around her pale face. He didn't have to see her expression to know she was angry.

"I don't know for sure but probably Sunrise Camp. When the shooting started, I saw her run off with Sol and a bunch of the others."

"What's Sunrise Camp?"

"The other Seeker camp.

"Let's go!" she said eagerly.

"I wish we could, but I don't know how to get there on foot in the dark, and taking the road's too risky at this point." He didn't mention that besides the angry loggers, Heller and any number of drug runners could be out there patrolling the dirt roads through the National Forest.

Hanks' attack on Harmony had been a complete surprise to him, but maybe Fox and Heller being at Logjammers had triggered it. Hanks had good reason to be concerned that the Seekers and their illegal marijuana operation might draw the attention of law enforcement to the area. It would expose his own illegal logging to public scrutiny.

Zoe's voice cut through his thoughts. "Why didn't you go with them?"

"I wanted to make sure you were safe."

That seemed to satisfy her, because for a moment she

was quiet. She turned her face up to the sky. In the pale light of the moon, the interplay of illumination and shadows accentuated her striking features. Jason inhaled the cold night air and redirected his attention back to the matter at hand.

"It's getting cold and will keep getting colder until dawn. Let's see if Hanks is done trashing Harmony. Maybe we can find a usable blanket or two."

"And my purse," she added.

He led her through the trees, avoiding the footpath, as they made their way back through the forest to Harmony. The acrid smell of burning plastic reached them long before they got close enough to see what was left of the camp. They hid in the shadows of the redwood grove and watched Hanks and his buddies, who stood around the clearing looking bored. There was nothing left to trash.

"I need more beer." Hanks waved his flashlight around haphazardly. "Let's go." He lurched down the trail to the parking lot, followed by the others.

They left smoldering destruction in their wake.

#

Please be here!

Zoe raced across the clearing, hoping the loggers had been too drunk to notice her purse. The moment she saw the smoking ashes of what had been the picnic tables, she knew it was futile. How could she take Clare to the doctor, much less get home, without any credit cards or ID?

Shadow came up beside her. "Maybe they took your purse with them. Were you carrying a lot of cash?"

"Not much, but it had my cell phone and credit cards

in it." A sinking sensation hit her and she sat down on the ground as Shadow searched the area.

Her gun was gone. Worse, Hanks and his friends had her gun, and now they knew where she lived. An uncomfortable and unfamiliar feeling of defeat coursed through her. Maybe it was an aftereffect of the adrenaline or because she'd been running on empty for so long that she'd finally gotten to the end of her rope, but tears clouded her eyes. She swiped at them impatiently. She hadn't cried in years. She wasn't about to start.

"Now what?" she said, trying to keep her voice neutral.

"Don't worry, we'll find your sister and the others in the morning."

"Where can we sleep? They burned everything." She winced when she heard the despair in her voice, but she was suddenly too exhausted to care if she sounded like a wimp.

"Come on." Shadow held out a hand.

She took it and let him hoist her to her feet. He gave her hand a gentle squeeze.

"I couldn't find any usable blankets, but that's OK. We don't need them."

There was something in his voice, some compassionate note of sympathy that made her look up at him. He was a tall, dark presence, his face a black, unreadable silhouette, hidden by his beard and shaggy hair.

Somewhere in a tree far above an owl hooted. Except for that one lonely sound, the silence was absolute. She was very aware of the fact that it was just the two of them, alone in the night. She shivered from cold, from exhaustion, and from the unexpected intimacy of the moment.

"We need to trust each other if we're going to get through the night, OK?" Shadow brushed the hair away from her face.

She jerked back fast. "I'm not afraid of you."

And she wasn't, she realized, despite having just met the guy.

"Good," he continued. "I hear a creek up ahead. Let's get water there and find a place to sleep nearby."

Water. What with everything else going on, thirst had been the last thing on her mind. Now, her mouth felt bone dry.

She followed him a short distance to a small creek. It meandered through the forest across a bed of smooth, flat rocks.

"Probably better filtered, but under the circumstances--" He knelt, rinsed his hands where the water ran freely across one of the rocks, and then moved slightly upstream to a small pool where he scooped up water and sipped from his cupped hands.

She followed suit, her hands instantly going numb when she submerged them in the pool. The water was so cold it hurt her teeth. She drank greedily. It was refreshing, despite the earthy taste.

"This should do." Shadow's voice came from nearby. He was using his boots to kick aside a mass of fallen branches.

"For what?" she asked, walking over to him.

"We'll sleep here."

She grimaced, trying not to think about what bugs might be crawling around in the dirt. "I guess a shower and a nice soft bed are out?"

"Not tonight, I'm afraid. How about a rain check?" he chuckled.

She didn't think responding was a good idea. Instead,

she watched him smooth out an area big enough for the two of them. He covered it with a thick layer of redwood pine needles and small branches.

"Ready for bed?" He turned to her.

"Um," Zoe paused, embarrassed. "I've got to use the bushes. I'll be right back."

"Me, too."

The instant she stepped away from him, the immensity of the night closed in on her. Her feet made just the slightest of sounds, muffled by the spongy material covering the forest floor. There was something eerie about being surrounded by so much silent darkness. It was nothing like the City or the desert, where there was always the bright moon or stars, and there was almost always a wind moving, stirring the air. Didn't Clare find it weird, maybe scary, too? No way did she want to be left alone in this place.

She hurried back to where Shadow had already lain down on the ground, but then stopped, struck by t.he realization that she was about to sleep with a stranger.

"This isn't so bad." He patted the ground beside him.

She glanced around the dark forest, filled with endless trees and drunken lunatics and who knew what else. Given the situation, this was a lot better than the alternative.

Well, here goes nothing, she thought as she lay down beside him.

She looked up at the narrow crack of sky, far above the treetops. It had been years since she'd slept under the open sky, and never alone with a man other than her dad, but she was too physically uncomfortable to think long about that. The ground was hard and lumpy. The cold crept up from the earth below and the icy air descended like a heavy weight. Her toes were numb inside her boots. A shiver ran through her. In seconds, her teeth started chattering.

"Roll onto your side." Shadow's voice broke the quiet stillness.

"I'm freezing, and my feet are wet."

"Take off your boots."

She didn't like taking orders, but under the circumstances, she didn't argue. She sat up and yanked off her boots. He did the same and then pulled branches over their legs.

"These will help." he said. "Now roll over and put your feet on my shins."

She did as he said and heard him inhale sharply as she placed her feet on him.

"You are cold," he said.

His shins were so warm they felt like they were on fire. She slid her feet along his shins, absorbing the wonderful heat. He settled more branches over their bodies and slid one arm under her neck, the other came to rest lightly across her waist. She tensed.

"Relax, I'm not making a move," he whispered through her hair. "W need to keep each other warm."

His body was a giant furnace compared to the vast cold of the forest around them. Merciful warmth seeped into her bones, but her brain spun with everything that had happened and with what she'd have to do the next day.

"There's no way Clare and I can make her appointment with the doctor tomorrow. I've gotta find a phone to call their office. And I need to call the insurance company about my car. I'll have to call my credit card companies, too." How could she get back to work on Monday without a car?

"We'll get out of here tomorrow. We'll find your

sister. Don't worry." Shadow's voice rumbled against her, its deep tones vaguely hypnotic and surprisingly comforting.

She closed her eyes and told herself to relax. A complex collection of scents, of cold night, dust and forest, of patchouli and man, filled her nose. Except for Shadow's rhythmic breath wafting into her hair and the sound of her own blood rushing in her ears, the night was totally silent.

Who would've thought when she woke up this morning that she'd be spending the night with a hippie on the bare ground in the middle of nowhere? Her job, her apartment, her whole life in the City seemed a million miles away.

***

CHAPTER FIVE

Early Morning, Saturday, Humboldt Forest

Jason's shoulder twinged. He tried shifting his position where he lay on the hard ground, but his arm was pinned under a woman's neck. She was warm and her hair smelled of lemons and orange blossoms, of spring and happy times.

So good.

He pulled her closer. Her body fit perfectly against his. He reached under her coat, needing to feel her skin. His hand met silky hot flesh that burned.

"Your hand's freezing!" The woman grabbed his hand and yanked it away from her body. She struggled out of his arms and sat up.

Reality rushed back to him. He'd just spent the night with Clarity's sister, Zoe Thompson. He rolled onto his back and tucked his hands behind his head, stretching. He looked up at her.

"How did you sleep?" he asked.

"OK, surprisingly." Her curly, auburn-red hair stood up in a wild tangle all over her head and her mascara had smudged. It gave her a sultry, sexy look. "I'll be back." She got up and disappeared into the forest.

Jason sat up and ran his hands through his shaggy hair. He couldn't wait to cut the damned stuff off once this assignment was over.

Darkness still reigned under the forest canopy. He looked up at the small bright patch of sky way above the redwoods. He guessed it was about 7 a.m. He'd stopped wearing a watch since going undercover with the Seekers. Sol believed in what he called "Natural Time" and living by the sun rather than human-designated hours. Like watches, cell phones were also rejected by the Seekers, so Jason kept his burner a secret.

Hunger clawed his gut. He ignored it and pushed himself off the ground and headed to the trees in the opposite direction from Zoe. He was back by the time she reappeared.

"So how're we going to find Clare?" She looked at him eagerly.

"Let's head to Woodsville so you can make your calls. Maybe we can catch a ride to Sunrise Camp." He also needed to call Porter and let him know about Hanks destroying Harmony.

"How?" she asked.

He gazed down into her bright, inquisitive face. She was way too perceptive, which could mean trouble down the road. For the length of a heartbeat, he considered breaking cover. They'd known each other less than twenty-four hours, but it didn't feel right lying to her.

Laying on his Seeker cover, he gave an indifferent shrug. "Gotta go with the flow, Pele. Trust the process. It'll work out."

"That's your plan, 'Go with the flow?'" She scowled at him. "Enough talking, let's go."

He led the way through the forest. His senses were alive to the woman following him as much as to the land around them. She kept surprising him. Last night, he'd written her off as a bossy, high-maintenance woman, but after a night on the cold, hard ground, she hadn't once complained.

Thinking about last night, Jason wondered again about Derrick Hanks destroying Harmony. Except for carousing at Logjammers, Hanks usually kept a low profile, wanting to keep his illegal logging activities off the public radar. Legitimate logging didn't pay like it used to and Hanks couldn't afford to lose his only source of extra income. The Seekers were easy targets and not likely to press charges, but something must have happened to goad Hanks and his buddies enough to make the long drive up to Harmony.

Whatever it was, Jason bet it had to do with the uneasy relations between the loggers and Heller and the vast stretch of forestland. Until assigned to this case, he hadn't understood exactly how much crime lay hidden among the big trees and secret clearings of the Humboldt National Forest. Maybe when he called in, his boss could shed some light on the situation.

He glanced over his shoulder at Zoe. She was climbing over a fallen tree. She was a trouper, no doubt about it. And she must really love her sister to be willing to go to such lengths for her.

#

Zoe followed Shadow across the uneven ground, amazed at how smoothly he navigated the rough terrain. He moved like he'd spent his whole life in the forest.

She remembered the instant when she first awoke, before he'd put his icy hand on her belly. In that brief moment, despite the hard ground cutting into her hip and shoulder, she'd felt a strange feeling of rightness and belonging in his arms, as if she'd finally come home after a long journey.

Enough of that, she mentally shook herself. Sentimentality wasn't her style. Neither were hippies.

For the umpteenth time, she wondered if Clare was OK, especially after all the crazed mayhem last night. Had Clare made it safely to Sunrise Camp? Zoe still couldn't believe she'd had to dodge bullets.

Shadow's plan to go back to Woodsville didn't seem like much of one, but at least she'd be able to get to a phone and call her insurance and credit card companies, as well as the doctor in Garberville. Maybe she could figure out a way to get some cash, too.

Hunger chewed on her stomach like a hundred gnawing rats. She hated being hungry and usually kept a few energy bars in her purse for just such occasions, but she'd eaten both on the long drive yesterday. Her purse was history, anyway.

"You don't have any money on you?" she asked Shadow.

"Five bucks, I think."

Not much, but enough to get something to eat in Woodsville.

They stepped out of the dim forest and into the bright daylight shining on a dirt road.

"Here's our road," Shadow said.

"How did you know it was here?"

"We headed south last night, so I knew if we reversed direction and headed north, we'd cross it."

His logical explanation seemed at odds with his earlier Seeker-casual attitude. She wondered about his contradictory personality as they descended the steep road down the mountain.

A deep, rasping call echoed through the trees. Zoe looked up. A large black bird was perched on a branch directly above them. It looked like a crow, but much larger. Was it a raven? Dark, beady eyes stared uncannily back at her. There was something strangely purposeful in the bird's unblinking gaze. She stumbled.

"You OK?" Shadow caught her arm.

She grasped his hand as she regained her footing. "You see that bird?" She pointed to the branch overhead.

"What bird?"

She looked up. The raven was gone.

I've got to get out of here, she thought.

She was being ridiculous, getting scared off by a bird, but no amount of rationalizing could stop her sudden need to flee. She wanted out of the dark, shadowy forest and back to a place like the deserts she was used to, with wide open vistas where she could see what was coming from miles away.

Shaking off his hand, she started to run, feeling pursued by a dark, malevolent presence.

"What's wrong?" Shadow ran after her.

"I don't know, but I feel like we're being watched."

"Then let's get out of sight."

He pulled her with him off the road and behind a big tree. He froze, listening intently. She strained to hear something beyond the blood pounding in her ears and their hushed breaths floating on the cold morning air.

Nothing.

No crunch of feet on the dirt road, no sudden beat of wings overhead. Whatever it was she'd thought was watching them was gone, or had she simply imagined it?

"There's no one there." He studied her for a long, silent moment, his green eyes narrowed and serious.

He probably thinks you've lost your mind, she thought, breaking eye contact with him.

Her hands were numb with cold. She shoved them into her jacket pockets.

"I'm guess I'm just being paranoid," she said.

Shadow tucked a finger under her chin and tilted her face up, his hand warm on her skin. "It's natural to feel a jumpy after what you've been through, Pele."

"My name is Zoe." She hated that stupid Seeker name, but she didn't move away from him. There was something so astute, so perceptive in his gaze. It made her feel naked, but safe at the same time.

"Don't discount your instincts, Zoe. You should trust them. Sometimes they're your best guide."

His hand left her chin and smoothed over her hair briefly before dropping away. Their eyes met. She felt a flush creep up her face.

He continued, "It's crucial to distinguish between the real, external threats and our own internal fears. There can be times when our lives may depend on it."

"Are you trying to make me feel better or worse?"

"Just speaking the truth." Shadow turned away and continued leading her down the steep dirt road.

They descended into a stand of gigantic trees that lined each side of the road. The air grew colder and the light darker under the towering trees.

"Wow!" She craned her neck upward. Somewhere way up there was the sunny morning.

"You've never seen old-growth redwoods before?"

"I grew up in Phoenix. The tallest thing we have in the desert is saguaro cactus."

"We're on the border of Humboldt Redwoods State Park. These are true old-growth redwoods, not second or third growth. Some can live more than two thousand years."

Zoe looked around at the redwoods with their looming heights and shaded light.

"It feels like I'm in a natural cathedral," she said.

"Doesn't it?" Shadow nodded. "Places like this have a special power."

"What do you mean?"

"This place stands outside human time. It transcends us and our own petty concerns."

"Is that what the Seekers believe?"

"Yes, but don't you, too?"

Zoe thought about it. Most of her life did seem trivial, compared to the grandeur of where they were walking.

"I get that feeling sometimes when I go running on the beach in San Francisco. There's something about that horizon, that border where the earth meets the sky. It seems to put everything into perspective."

"Right on," Shadow nodded. He gestured broadly to the forest around them. "Imagine what California must have been like before any of the redwoods were cut down."

The image of a wild country, untamed and primordial, rose up in her mind. Hiking inside the redwood cathedral, she could almost believe the forest stretched across the endless, undulating mountains and valleys, shadowing the land in its timeless twilight.

They hiked in reverent silence until they left the old-growth grove. Sunlight streamed down, bright and warm on them again. Shadow picked up the pace and broke into a jog. She hurried after him, thinking what an enigma he was. What kind of hippie ever ran anywhere?

"Why did you join the Seekers?" she called after him.

#

Jason slowed his pace to answer Zoe's question. "It's not a very exciting story," he shrugged.

"We've got time to kill, so enlighten me." She wasn't going to let it drop.

Like most good cover stories, his story stuck pretty close to the truth, minus a few of the more salient details.

He summarized quickly. "In a nutshell, my life was falling apart. I grew up around here, so I came back. I was hoping to reconnect with my youth, or at least the idealism I used to feel when I was young. Bottom line, I was looking for a deeper, more meaningful purpose. Anyway, I met Sol. He changed everything for me. He gave me a whole new vision for how to live my life." He sent her a glance laden with what he hoped looked like heartfelt meaning.

"You're kidding." She gave him a skeptical look.

"No, I'm not. The dude's brilliant," he said, breaking into a jog again.

He wasn't lying about Sol. The man was charismatic, a born leader. The more time Jason spent with him, the more he understood how Sol had built such a following. Too bad Sol's message centered on marijuana.

What he still didn't understand, though, was how Sol could be in league with Rob Heller. It just didn't make sense. Heller was a soulless profiteer and sadist, who didn't care who he destroyed in his single-minded pursuit of power, be it money or sex, whereas Sol was the epitome of an idealist, who mistakenly believed he was helping mankind by growing top quality marijuana. Jason hadn't uncovered any evidence to indicate that Sol profited financially from growing marijuana. The man lived with his fellow commune members like paupers, in the most Spartan of lifestyles.

"Are you and my sister involved?" Zoe asked.

Whatever he'd been expecting her to ask, it wasn't that. "Excuse me?"

"Did you follow her up here? Is that the real reason you joined the Seekers?"

"No."

"It wouldn't be the first time."

"What?"

"You can't deny she's beautiful. Ever since we were kids, she's had guys following after her."

"You are, too."

"I'm no Clare."

Zoe was right about that. Where Clarity had an ephemeral beauty, a kind of otherworldly, spiritual air, Zoe was all fire, hot energy, and action. When he'd touched her first thing in the morning, her skin had almost burned his hand. He clenched his fist.

"Clarity and I are just friends," he said, wanting to reassure her. "You're way more capable." The moment he said it, he knew it sounded lame.

"That's me, eminently capable." She didn't smile.

"It's good to be capable." Better to hurt her feelings than let on how much she affected him.

They reached the paved road to Woodsville. They stepped out of the forest into bright morning sunshine.

#

Was he telling the truth? Zoe wondered as they walked into Woodsville.

Had he really joined the Seekers looking for inspiration? It sounded plausible enough. What did it matter if he and Clare were involved, anyway? She should be glad Clare was finally involved with someone who seemed at least halfway competent, even if he was a pot-smoking Seeker.

In the light of day, Woodsville was even less impressive than it had been last night. Paint peeled from the sun-faded clapboard storefronts. The main street was deserted of both cars and people, but maybe that was because it was still early on a Saturday morning. Zoe followed Shadow to the gas station and mini-mart.

"The payphone's over there." Shadow pointed toward the side of the building.

"Food first," Zoe said.

She walked to the mini-mart's front door and pushed it open. A bell tinkled as she went in. Shadow followed her inside.

"Good morning." A rail thin young woman behind the register smiled at her.

"You wouldn't happen to know anything about a group called the Seekers or a place called 'Sunrise Camp,' would you?" Zoe asked, hoping to get lucky.

"I've heard of them, but that's all I know. Sorry." The cashier's eyes moved to Shadow.

"Jason Parrish, is that you? JoAnn said you were back. You let your hair grow." The cashier came around the register and threw her arms around Shadow.

"Shelley." His voice was muffled in her sweater as she hugged him. "I thought you worked at the mini-mart down in Garberville."

Was "Jason" his real name?

66

Zoe watched Shadow step back from the cashier and smile at the woman. The smile stopped Zoe short. She'd never seen him smile like that, open and warm. She realized that despite his unkempt appearance and grungy clothes, he wasn't unattractive.

"I'm pinch-hitting for Audrey while she's out with the flu," the cashier said. She smiled brightly at him. It was obvious she liked Shadow, or Jason, or whatever his name was. Really liked him.

Zoe cut in. "I'm going to get some coffee and some food. You want some?"

"No thanks," Shadow said. He stayed at the counter and chatted with the cashier.

Zoe went to the junk food rack and grabbed a couple of energy bars. She then went to the beverage area and got the coffee. She brought the items back to the counter.

"That'll be $5.50," the cashier said, looking at Zoe curiously.

Shadow didn't offer any introductions. He smoothed a crumpled bill on the counter and seemed eager to get out of there. "All we've got is a five."

"For you, Jase, anything." The cashier gave him another of her too-friendly smiles.

"We owe you one, Shel," he said.

Zoe opened one of the energy bars, but Shadow was already out the door before she'd taken a bite. She rushed after him.

"This is yours." She tried to hand him the other energy bar.

"Keep it." He kept his hands in his jacket pockets. His eyes traveled up and down the street, as if he was looking for something.

"You paid for it. Aren't you starving?"

"Sure, but no worries."

"You sure?" He had to be starving; she was.

He looked back at her and shook his head. "I can wait."

The way he said the words and the look he gave her made her heart jump, and it wasn't from the caffeine. Maybe the lack of sleep and aftereffects of last night's adrenaline were playing tricks with her hormones. He wasn't her type.

"Your real name is Jason?"

"My name is Shadow." His eyes glinted.

"How do you know that woman?" The question was out before she realized it sounded a little too much like she cared.

"Shelley's a friend of my older sister, JoAnn. I've known her since we were kids." His manner shifted and became all business. "Go make your calls. I'll be back in a half hour."

"Where are you going?"

"I'm gonna see if we can line up a ride to Sunrise Camp."

She wondered what he wasn't telling her, but it was time to take care of her own business. Half an hour wasn't a lot of time to make her calls, especially if she had trouble getting the numbers she needed from information. She headed to the phone booth.

#

Jason set off across the street toward Logjammers, cursing under his breath. It wasn't surprising that someone from Garberville would take extra work in Woodsville if they could get it, but if he'd known Shelley would be at the mini-mart, he'd have let Zoe go in alone.

He ducked down the alley and entered Logjammers through the back door. He needed to talk to Charlie, who had a bead on anyone coming through Woodsville. Maybe the old bartender could shed some light on Hanks' behavior last night. He also had to check in with his boss.

Jason passed along the hallway stacked high with boxes of empty beer bottles ready for recycling. The place smelled of booze and stale cigarette smoke, with the faint hint of urine. It reminded him of the countless trips to Logjammers he used to make with his dad, when his dad was still alive and in between logging jobs, looking to raise hell somewhere far enough from home that he wouldn't catch hell when he got home. Jason first learned to fight in one those drunken brawls his dad liked to incite when he was boozing.

A pan crashed in the kitchen. Jason went inside and found Charlie standing at the sink with his back to him. He tapped the white-haired man on the shoulder.

"Charlie?"

The old man put down the pan he was washing and turned around. He squinted at Jason. "Who wants to know?"

"Jason Parrish. Remember, Richard Parrish's boy?"

Recognition flashed across the man's grizzled face. He gave Jason the once over as he dried his hands on the dishtowel tucked in his apron.

"You need a haircut, boyo. I heard you came back, but what the hell you doing, joining up with that hippie cult? They're nothing but drugs and all kinds of trouble, and not one of them can hold down a decent job." He scowled, his white shaggy brows bristling. "Weren't you with the police down south? Why'd you leave something respectable like that. Your kid sister—"

"It's a long story," Jason cut him off before he started in about Tammy.

Jason crossed the kitchen to the swinging door leading to the bar and peeked through. The place was empty. He turned back to Charlie, who was watching him with interest.

"Want some coffee?" the old guy asked.

Zoe had offered him some at the mini-mart, but to keep cover with her, he'd had to decline, since Seekers disdained stimulants. He hadn't had any coffee since going undercover and was jonesing for a good jolt. Keeping cover with Charlie wasn't so important. The old guy could keep a secret.

"You're a savior, Charlie. Got any food to spare, too? I can't pay you right now, but I'm good for it."

"Son, yer daddy would turn over in his grave if I didn't feed you when you was hungry."

Charlie poured him a steaming mug of coffee. Jason sipped the dark brew. It was fresh, hot, and good. *This* was a drug he could use.

Charlie pulled open the oversized door of the commercial fridge and removed a stack of packaged meats.

"Can you make it fast?" Jason asked, taking another swig of the coffee.

"You in some kind of trouble?" Shrewd eyes measured him.

"No trouble. You know why Derrick Hanks is crazy mad at the Seekers right now? Something set him off?"

Charlie looked up from assembling a hefty sandwich. "When's he not pissed at them? Ever since Sol got them growing weed in the forest, he's been mad. But it's also that time of year again and the hordes of hippies are showing up. Those damned druggies. They mean nothing but trouble for us law abiding folk. Present company excluded, I hope?"

Jason clenched his jaw. It sucked having to lie to his dad's old friend. "Just because someone dresses a certain way doesn't mean they break the law. Other people break laws, too, like Hanks and his crew."

"Loggers are on tough times these days," Charlie scowled. "Things ain't like they used to be, not like when your daddy was alive. Them damned environmentalists, those government bureaucrats, they—"

"Can you to do something else for me?" Jason interrupted the old man's tirade.

"I don't know, boyo. Maybe I should whip your ass for joining that cult and dishonoring your daddy's memory." Charlie thrust the giant sandwich at him.

"I'd like to see you try." Jason grinned and tucked the sandwich into his jacket pocket.

Charlie scratched his beard and looked at him warily. "What you need?"

"Couple of things. Can you keep it confidential?"

"You have to ask me that, boyo? Don't you know your daddy came down here to Logjammers all those times because he knew I'd never rat to your ma?"

"Keep your eyes and ears open for names and faces."

"I always do."

"Rob Heller—"

"That snooty, no-good, lazy ass—"

"Hey Charlie," a man called from the front room and interrupted Charlie's pithy assessment of Heller's character. "You back there?"

Jason stepped back, out of sight along the kitchen wall.

Charlie peered under the warmer lamps to the barroom. "'Morning, Jack. The usual?"

"Yup," the man answered.

71

"Coming right up," Charlie called out. He turned to Jason and dropped his voice. "Jack's the mailman. He stops in for a bite most mornings." He cracked a couple eggs onto the griddle. The smell of sizzling butter filled the air.

"One more thing, Charlie. Can I borrow your phone?"

"Sure."

"Thanks, Charlie, for everything." Jason finished his coffee and set the empty mug in the large stainless steel sink. "I'll check back with you in a few days. Remember, anything about Heller, you let me know." Jason started for the back door.

"I'll help you if you promise me something," Charlie called after him.

Jason stopped in his tracks and looked back over his shoulder.

"You leave that hippie cult and clean up your act, you hear? You and your sister JoAnn are the good kids. God knows your older brother's a lost cause, and well, Tammy, God rest her soul. You promise me!"

"On Tammy's memory." Jason nodded and left the kitchen.

He headed outside and up the wooden stairs to Charlie's apartment over the bar. He let himself into the unlocked apartment and crossed over to where an old rotary phone sat on a rolltop desk covered in stacks of bills and business documents. He picked up the receiver and dialed his calling card number. His boss didn't pick up, so he left Porter a quick update on voicemail.

***

CHAPTER SIX

10 a.m. Saturday, Woodsville

Zoe hung up the payphone at the Woodsville mini-mart. She drained the last of her now-cold coffee and wondered where Jason was. She had to remind herself to still call him Shadow. She'd much rather call him by his real name, but he insisted on the pretentious Seeker name.

A paint-splattered van pulled into the gas station. She recognized the driver's long, flowing blond hair. It was Fox. He was talking on a cell phone, but when he saw her, the phone disappeared. She hurried across the parking lot to where he was pumping gas. He was looking at himself in the van window's reflection and running his free hand through his hair.

"Hey, do you know where my sister Clare is?" she asked.

He turned and his blue eyes traveled over her briefly, before he nodded and said something that sounded like "Jaaaahhhman."

"What does that mean?" she said impatiently.

He finished gassing the van and hung up the pump before answering. "Clarity's with Sol. We all went to Sunrise Camp last night, everybody except you two," he said as Shadow walked up.

"Dude, that so totally sucked at Harmony last night." Shadow shook his head dramatically. He spoke very differently to Fox than he did to her when they were alone. "Ya' goin' to Sunrise Camp anytime soon? Pele needs to talk to Clarity."

"Jahman, leaving now. Wanna lift?"

Minutes later, they trundled out of Woodsville in the old rattletrap van. Zoe looked around for a seat belt in the back seat, but if the van had once had rear belts, they were long gone. Fox lit up a joint. Not using a seatbelt didn't seem nearly as illegal as Fox driving while puffing away on a joint, but she wasn't going to turn down the ride, no matter how bumpy and uncomfortable it was. The van had lousy suspension, but it beat hiking all the way to Sunrise Camp, and it would get them there a whole lot faster.

"Where'd ja go last night?" Fox asked Shadow, who was sitting in the front passenger seat. Fox steered the van with one hand, with the other, he held the joint delicately between his thumb and forefinger.

"We spent the night out."

"On the ground?" Fox released a stream of pungent smoke out the open window.

It blew straight back in the rear window and into Zoe's face. She coughed and slid over on the bench seat.

"Bummer uncomfortable, dude." Fox handed Shadow the joint.

Zoe stared in anger. They still hadn't found Clare. Now was *not* the time to be getting high, but then she remembered. He was a Seeker—that's what they did.

Shadow took a big drag on the joint and then waved it back to Zoe.

"Hey, Pele, you wanna hit?"

"No thanks." Until she got her sister safely to medical help, she couldn't relax. Getting stoned would just make her anxiety more intense.

Shadow handed the joint back to Fox. "What brought you into town?"

"I needed to get some generators and stuff."

Zoe looked over the back seat. Several large plastic tanks were secured with straps to the inside walls of the van, along with a bunch of equipment and what looked like electric lights.

"Generators?" Shadow asked. "I thought Sol wanted to keep everything natural."

"Jahman, but we've gotta be prepared, dude. If the weather changes, we might have to work all night during harvest. I got some high-powered lights."

"Is there a harvest date?"

"Not yet, but ja ask me, Sol's cutting it close. The shit's already primo, man, but Sol says we gotta wait. He says it's not yet reached the max."

"He believes in perfection." Shadow nodded emphatically.

"That he does, man, the perfect bud." Fox finished the joint and flicked it out the window.

Shadow pulled something bulky from his coat pocket. "I've got the munchies." He unwrapped the package and the van filled with the rich, savory smells of a submarine sandwich.

"Dude, is that meat?" Fox said, sounding surprised.

"Someone offered it to me. No point being rude, and I'm starving." Shadow took a monster bite and chomped the sandwich. He looked over his shoulder at Zoe. "Want some?"

"Yes!" Zoe said. The energy bars and coffee from the mini-mart were a distant memory.

When Shadow handed the sub back to her, she saw the look in his eyes and did a double take. His eyes were half-closed with a look of ecstasy as he chewed.

Hadn't he said he was a vegetarian like the other Seekers? Why hadn't he removed the meat before digging in?

But she forgot the questions as she looked at the big sandwich in her hands and her stomach growled. She took a bite. It was chock full of deli meats. Flavors burst in her mouth. Whoever made it had put in everything but the kitchen sink. Under normal circumstances, she might have found the thing disgusting, but right now, it hit the spot. She took a few more big bites and then handed it back to Shadow.

"Thanks, I'm good," she said.

"Sure you don't want some?" Shadow asked Fox.

Fox glanced at the half-eaten sub and then nodded. "Ja, man. Righteous."

Zoe watched the two of them finish off the sandwich. Weren't they being hypocrites? "I thought the Seekers were vegetarian."

Shadow nodded. "Totally, but Sol also teaches us to 'Waste not, want not.'"

Time to get the conversation back on track. "How far is it to Sunrise Camp?" she asked.

"Almost there," Fox said, spinning the wheel as the van rounded a tight switchback.

#

Jason crumpled the sub wrapper and hid it under the van's front seat. No point flaunting his carnivorous cravings in front of the more devout Seekers. From his surveillance work, he knew Fox had few morals. He hadn't had the heart to tell Charlie to hold the meat. He was damned tired of eating nuts and berries. Now, thanks to Charlie's handiwork, his belly felt more satisfied than it had in days.

The sandwich had also erased the marijuana taste from his mouth. He'd long ago mastered the art of drawing smoke into his mouth without actually inhaling, but Zoe didn't know that. He'd seen her face her face when he'd smoked the joint. It sucked disappointing her, but he had to do it to keep his cover with Fox, and with her. She was getting way too suspicious.

They reached the top of the long climb where the mountain leveled off and the dirt road ended at the parking area. The sun shone hot on the clear-cut land. Fox stopped the van and they climbed out. Two Seekers Jason recognized came out of the forest.

"Dudes, why aren't you at the garden?" Fox said to the two men.

"Sol wanted us to catch some z's, 'cause we're on night watch after what happened at Harmony. We heard the van and thought we'd better make sure it was you."

Zoe shifted impatiently beside Jason. "Can we get going?"

He understood her impatience, but he knew from experience that she'd get nowhere fast by pushing the Seekers. He introduced the big, black bearded guy and the shorter, blonde one. "Bear and Smiley, this is Clarity's sister, Pele."

"You're Clarity's sister, huh? How cool is that!" Bear wrapped Zoe in a hug.

Jason grinned as Zoe squirmed in the guy's brawny arms. She'd made a fan.

"Sol named her Pele, you know, the Hawaiian Goddess of Fire," Fox said, pointing to Zoe's hair when she pulled free of Bear.

Her curly hair had gotten even wilder from the windy van ride. It stood up all over her head. With its red highlights, Jason could almost picture it as some kind of fiery lava.

"Awesome, Goddess of Fire." Bear had eyes only for Zoe.

"Do you know where Clare is?" Zoe asked.

"We'll take you there, 'cause your wish is my command, Goddess." Bear grinned at Zoe.

Jason and Zoe followed the others on the footpath to Sunrise Camp. Jason recognized a few of the tents from his last trip there, but now tarps had been strung between trees to create even more sleeping areas, with pads and blankets strewn about under them. With Harmony destroyed, it was clear the Seekers were hard-pressed for gear. It looked like most of the Seekers had been reduced to dog-piling and sleeping outside.

"Where's Clare?" Zoe asked, looking around the deserted camp.

"She's at the garden." Bear tried to hide a massive yawn behind his hand.

"The garden?" Zoe asked.

"Where we grow the most awesome, spectacular cannabis," Fox said. "I'll take you there."

"See ya soon, Goddess," Bear said, before flopping down on a blanket near where Smiley had already lain down.

Jason and Zoe followed Fox to the grow.

#

A strange, low-pitched sound resonated eerily through the forest and grew louder as Zoe and Shadow followed Fox through the forest.

"What's that sound?" she asked.

"The universal 'Om,'" Fox said over his shoulder.

"The what?"

Fox stopped and turned around. "Whoa, dude, like you never heard the chant 'Om' before?" He looked at her in shock, his eyes red from the joint he'd smoked.

"No." What she heard sounded nothing like the word "Om."

"Sol says when you chant 'Om,' you merge all energy and all forms, everything, from the most gross to the most divine. It's freakin' powerful." Fox flipped his long blond hair over his shoulders with both hands.

"Totally." Shadow nodded like he really believed all that New Age stuff.

Zoe scowled at him as they started walking again. She wanted to think of him as Jason, as someone she could relate to, like when they were alone together, but he was a Seeker. Shadow was his true identity.

The trail ended and the redwood forest dropped away. Sloping gently downward and away to the south spread a field of tall, bushy plants, planted closely together in narrow rows. Most were as tall as she was, with some noticeably bigger, maybe six feet high or more. She had no idea how many plants there were, but there had to be at least a thousand. She'd never seen a pot plant before. The intense afternoon sun intensified the pungent, sage-like smell of the plants. The odor was almost overpowering as it wafted up the hill on the hot, dry breeze.

"Is that pot?" she asked.

Fox spread his arms wide. "Yes, isn't it beautiful? Sol knows all the magic secrets for growing the best fucking cannabis in the world."

She ignored him and looked around for Clare. Guys stood at regular intervals along the border of the pot field, each standing about ten feet apart from each other. They were all chanting "Om" in deep voices, but there was no break in sound. Voices would start up as others faded away, a continuous tonal wave. She didn't see her sister anywhere.

"We're helping the cannabis grow," Shadow said.

"By chanting at them?" Zoe tried not to roll her eyes. The whole thing looked and sounded ridiculous.

"The plants feel the vibrations of the universal 'Om.' They respond to it and grow faster, better," Shadow explained.

Sol came out of one row of the plants. He was smiling serenely and held something carefully in one hand.

"Is that what I think it is?" Shadow asked.

Fox rushed forward and took the thing from Sol. He held it up and closely examined it. The thing looked like some sort of small, weird plant.

"Holy shit, man, this is the fattest looking bud I've ever seen!" Fox said, a rapt and ravenous expression on his face.

"Beautiful, isn't she?" Sol sounded like a proud father. "Our loving care is beginning to reap rewards, my friends. This is the first bud of our new crop."

Zoe couldn't care less about the damned crop. She stepped in front of Sol and pointed at Fox. "He told me you know where my sister is."

"My heart is glad to see that you and Shadow are safe after all of last night's troubles." Sol smiled warmly and held out his arms to her.

She refused the embrace, crossing her arms over her chest. She frowned, sick and tired of all the touchy-feely stuff. "Where's Clare?"

"Ah, it is good to feel your fire again, Pele." Sol studied her face with wide blue eyes. "Clarity is safe, do not worry. Luna has taken the women to the Retreat, because tomorrow night is the full moon."

"No—"

Sol interrupted her, "Have you never felt that special woman's connection with the moon?"

"What?"

"I suppose there are some feminine mysteries that must be taught. Luna teaches our Seeker women these profound truths. She takes them to a sacred place, deep in the heart of the forest during the full moon. There they practice the secret rituals."

Zoe couldn't believe Clare was gone again. She was done being polite. "I need to find Clare. Can you take me to her?"

"Do not fear, Pele, I will, but please, first join us in chanting the universal 'Om', the beginning and end, the original sound of the universe." Sol held out his hand to her.

"Didn't you hear what I just said?" She waved his hand away.

"Breathe, Pele, release your worry." Sol closed his eyes. "Finding Clarity is not all of your journey. Feel the forest. Om—"

Sol turned away and spread his arms to the field, as if embracing the entirety of it. His voice rose and blended with the other male voices, chanting the single word, their voices striving for a single tone. Fox had left to join the other chanting men, but Shadow still stood beside her.

"Can you take me to her?" she asked.

He shook his head. "I'm sorry, but none of us guys are allowed to the Retreat. I don't even know where it is."

Zoe looked up and saw how far the sun had moved across the sky. Saturday was quickly disappearing.

Shadow touched her shoulder and dipped his head closer so he could speak quietly to her over the chanting. "You can trust Sol. He'll take you to Clarity, but you have to be patient. He works by his own clock."

"This is nuts!" She wanted to stamp her foot in frustration.

"I'm sorry." Shadow gave her shoulder a gentle squeeze, but then he, too, began the chant.

The sun beat down and the day grew hotter. The air was humid and thick with the scent of growing plants. Zoe tried not to follow Sol's advice about breathing, because the intense odor of the pot, combined with the men's endless chanting, was making her feel light-headed and like she was getting a contact high.

Shadow turned to her. "You feeling OK?"

"Not really."

"Let's get you out of the sun."

"Thanks."

He led her to the edge of the forest, where she found a smooth place on the ground in the shade. She sat down and closed her eyes to stop the world from spinning.

#

All the hype around Sol's special magic with marijuana was well-deserved. Jason had never seen a bud as big, hairy, and potent-looking as the one Sol had showed them. As Jason chanted, he looked at the grow and realized that the all-female crop had spiked buds all over their branches. Fox was right. The harvest was fast approaching.

He glanced back to check on Zoe sitting at the edge of the forest. He noticed Rob Heller come out of the trees on the path from Sunrise Camp. Fortunately, Heller looked all business, with eyes only for the marijuana. He didn't notice Zoe.

Heller surveyed the grow like he owned it and then made a beeline for Sol, who stood chanting about ten feet from Jason. Jason stopped his own chanting so he could listen.

"We need to talk," Heller said loudly to Sol, who turned to him, his mouth still shaping the "Om."

Heller waved for Sol to follow him. They went back to the path to Sunrise Camp and disappeared into the forest. Jason glanced at the other chanting Seekers. Most had their eyes closed; all looked zoned out. Zoe sat with her eyes closed, too. Jason slipped between the trees.

Heller and Sol stood a short way along the trail. Jason kept behind one of the redwoods, but he could easily hear them over the chanting at the grow.

"Where are all the women?" Heller's voice rose angrily.

"Brock, your energy is red and yellow today, so turbulent, so wild." Sol spoke as he always did, slowly and calmly. "Your forceful badger nature has returned. Why have you waited so long to come to me? Our work together was helping restore harmony to your aura, but it has been some weeks now."

"I've been busy, old man," Heller said rudely.

"Breathe, Brock, breathe. Your rage will not change the way things are. It only destabilizes and weakens you. It makes you a victim of your circumstance."

"Cut the crap. Where the fuck is Clarity?"

Sol sighed audibly. There was a long pause.

Jason clenched his fists against the rage boiling up inside. No question, Heller's interest in Zoe's sister had morphed into obsession.

Sol started talking again. "The women have gone on Retreat for the full moon. They will return in three days, and—"

"Fuck!"

"As I was saying," Sol spoke over Heller, his tone still patient, as if speaking to a slow-witted student, "they will return in time for the harvest. Our plants are growing magnificently. Aren't they beautiful? Look at this, our first mature bud this year, do you see the trichomes? She promises potent medicine."

There was a pause and Jason risked looking around the tree. Heller was examining the bud.

"Now is not the time for half your workers to leave," he said.

"They'll be back, Brock. In the meantime, the plants are at a stage of maturation where they thrive on the deeper vibrations of male voices."

"We can't afford more trouble, not after what happened last night."

"That was unfortunate."

"Derrick Hanks is a drunk and a loose cannon."

"Poor man, he is a lost and misguided soul."

"I will not let him threaten the harvest." Heller's voice turned vicious.

"Brock, what are you planning?" Concern colored Sol's usually serene voice.

"Leave it to me, old man."

The exchange was winding down. Jason stole back to the grow, frustrated and worried by Heller's cryptic words.

#

Zoe stood in line with Shadow to get their bowls of vegetarian chili dinner. She was fuming about Sol.

"Don't worry, you'll get to see Clarity in the morning. Sol promised," Shadow said.

"You keep saying that, but so far all he's done is stall me."

Sol still hadn't offered a decent explanation for the delay, just that it was getting too late to make the hike to the Retreat.

She went with Shadow and their bowls of chili to stand near the bonfire where a bong was making the rounds. Wood smoke mixed in the air with drifting clouds of marijuana smoke. The combined smell wasn't unpleasant, but it infiltrated her clothes, her hair, every pore of her body. She yearned to breathe the clean air of the oncoming night.

"At least he's set a time to take you. That counts for something." Shadow took a bite of the chili.

"Maybe, but it's already Saturday night. I have to be at work on Monday. I can't afford to lose my job or my health insurance."

As soon as the words were out, she realized she was speaking to someone who cared nothing for calendar time, let alone the demands of a real job. One of the Seekers held a huge bong out to her. The thing was at least a foot high, made of dark, swirly glass with some kind of abstract pattern on it. The reservoir was the size of a small coffee pot.

"You need to chillax, babe," the Seeker said, breathing smoke out through his nostrils.

"No thanks." She shook her head decisively. No way was she going to put any more smoke into her lungs than she had to, much less get high with these guys. After what had happened last night, she wanted to keep her wits about her.

Sol watched her from his spot across the bonfire, his eyes bright in the firelight. "Your fire energy is strong, Pele, but you must not let it consume you."

"Right on, man," another guy murmured.

The bong passed her by and Shadow took it. She'd hoped he was different from the other Seekers and not just a glorified drug user, but so much for that idea. She ignored her renewed disappointment in him and focused on food. She took a bite of the chili. It was good and spicy. She wolfed it down.

Sol addressed the men sitting around the fire. "You are doing such excellent work, my friends, I commend you. The masculine energy of your voices, combined with the spirit of the redwoods and the water from this special mountain, will give these plants powers we can't yet imagine." He took the bong when it reached him. "This is going to be the best harvest yet, so let's keep up the good work for the next few days. I'd like to thank Cougar and Jay for volunteering to continue the chant overnight tonight and Bear and Smiley for keeping a look out on the road."

"When's harvest?" Fox asked.

Sol took a hit from the bong. Smoke streamed from his nose like a dragon. "I think another week, but just imagine, my friends, what we are doing here. We are growing the best, most powerful cannabis in the world, medicine that will relieve hundreds of people, perhaps more, from their suffering."

"Awesome!" "Right on." "Fucking yeah!" Seekers shouted their enthusiasm around the fire.

Zoe looked at Shadow sitting beside her as she finished her chili. Did he share their naive enthusiasm? His face was impassive, but his eyes were watering as he slowly ate the spicy food.

The bong made a few more rounds before the guys began cleaning up. Zoe followed Shadow over to a big plastic tub of water being used as a sink. They stood side by side and rinsed their bowls. The other Seekers were heading off to the various tent and tarp sleeping areas.

"You want to sleep with me again?" Shadow asked and then chuckled. "That didn't come out right, but you know what I mean."

She looked around and considered the options. What she really wanted was a shower and a clean, comfortable motel room, preferably with Clare sleeping in the bed next to hers.

"Come on, it'll be better than last night. We can even sleep on a pad instead of the ground. I found a good one over there." He pointed to the far corner of the camp.

She sure as heck didn't want to sleep with any of the other guys. At least he didn't stink too much.

"All right," she said and followed him to where the foam pad lay beneath a plastic tarp strung between several trees. The pad wasn't much wider than a single, but at least it was almost two inches thick.

Definitely better than sleeping on the ground, she thought as she fingered the ratty Mexican blanket, glad to find it was wool.

"No pillows?" she said, trying to lighten her mood, but she felt glum.

"You can use my arm again."

"It's hardly soft." She remembered how muscular he was under his baggy jacket.

"You don't have to, if you don't want to." He stretched out on his side of the pad.

She lay down beside him and listened to the night. No sound of gunshots or drunken men threatened, just a few crackles from the dying fire and the distant low tone of men chanting at the pot field. She still couldn't relax. Lying on her back, her head felt uncomfortably flat without a pillow.

After a few minutes, she broke the silence. "Is your offer still good?"

"Any time," he said quietly and rolled onto his side.

He stretched his arm out for her. She shifted into a comfortable position, lying with her head on his arm. The pad was thick enough to keep her hip bone cushioned from the ground. She wasn't quite spooning with him, but she could feel his body radiating heat. Warmth stole into her bones. For the first time all day, she began to relax.

"This is getting to be a habit," he whispered.

His breath teased the hair on the back of her neck. Instantly, every nerve of her body jumped awake, alive and attuned to him, his heat, his scent, and the hushed cadence of his breathing as it caressed her hair.

Dangerous. She forced her attention to something else, something she'd been wondering about.

"Why did you sneak away and follow Sol and that baldheaded guy this afternoon?"

She felt him tense, the muscles of his bicep flexing against her cheek where she lay. There was a pause before he spoke.

"Brock's trouble," he said.

"I met him last night at that bar in Woodsville." She remembered the unpleasant interchange. "He seemed like a creep. Fox was there. He called him 'Heller.'"

"His real name is Rob Heller, but Sol calls him 'Brock.'"

"'Brock'?" Zoe asked.

"Sol says it's an old Celtic term for 'badger,' an animal notorious for being a ferocious fighter. Brock's completely obsessed with money and the power that comes with it. He's using us for his own personal profit."

"I'm surprised Sol would do business with such a shark."

"Sol only sees the best in people."

"Isn't that naive?"

Shadow reached up and tucked her hair behind her ear. The gesture felt so good, she had to force herself to lie still and not lean into the comfort of his hand.

Don't be a naive fool, yourself, a small voice inside her warned. Shadow was just another Seeker.

"Let's get some sleep. Tomorrow's going to be a long day," he said, his voice low and quiet.

Zoe closed her eyes and told herself that tomorrow she'd get Clare to safety, but as she drifted off to sleep, she realized Shadow hadn't answered her question.

***

CHAPTER SEVEN

Sunday Morning, Sunset Camp

A bird call woke Zoe. The simple, two-note melody repeated for some time, resonating through the forest. She'd slept so well that it was almost a surprise to find herself lying in the middle of the forest under a blanket with a man she barely knew. Her life in San Francisco seemed very far away. For a moment, she didn't think about her sister and why she was there. She lay in Shadow's arms and listened.

"That's a black-capped chickadee calling for its mate." Shadow's voice came warm and intimate against her neck.

Too intimate.

"Time to get up," she said and disentangled herself from him.

Today was Sunday. She had to find Clare and get back to San Francisco by tonight. She got up from the sleeping pad and inhaled the crisp early morning air. It was filled with the scent of earth and forest. Sunrise Camp was beginning to stir with activity. Sol was lighting the camp fire, and Bear was starting the stove.

A short time later, while everyone was gathered around the morning fire eating their oatmeal, Zoe asked Sol, "When will you take me to Clare?"

"You will see Clarity today, but first, let's give thanks to the morning." Sol set his bowl on the ground and lifted his hands high overhead. He closed his eyes and tipped his head upward to the sky, his arms outspread. The other Seeker men followed suit.

Zoe watched with irritation. This felt like just one more delay in finding Clare. Somehow Sol knew without looking at her that she hadn't raised her arms.

"Please join us, Pele, please share our thanks for the new day," he said.

She didn't feel like being thankful or doing what Sol said, but she also didn't want to delay getting out of there by arguing with him. She lifted her arms up like everyone else.

The first rays of the sun pierced through the trees. She glanced at Shadow. Like the others, his face was tipped up to the sky and his eyes were closed. He looked peaceful and content. Despite his scraggly beard and messy hair, he looked good.

Good?

Mentally shaking herself, she closed her eyes. She felt the bright light of day warm on her face. In the quiet moment, standing like the others with her arms and face up to the morning sun, she was surprised to feel hope suddenly rising within her, washing away her irritation.

"Bless the light and the peace," Sol said. "Bless the serenity and truth of this land. Bless the power and strength of our minds and our bodies so that we may do good. Om—" he broke into the now familiar chant. The other men joined in.

When they finished, Zoe took Shadow aside. "Can you come with me to the Retreat?"

"Sorry, none of the men can go there except Sol." He took her hand in his. "You'll be OK. Sol would never harm anyone."

She looked down at their joined hands. "Will you be here when we get back?"

He gave her hand a gentle squeeze. "I'll be chanting the plants."

"Does that really work?"

"Sol thinks so." Shadow shrugged. "This is my first harvest, so I'll have to wait and see."

Sol approached, carrying a canvas duffel bag slung over his shoulder. "Come, Pele, it's time."

"See you soon." Shadow gave her a hug. "You're a good sister. Clarity's lucky to have you."

"Thanks," she said, turning to follow Sol.

She had to hurry to keep up with the Seeker leader as he strode away from Sunrise Camp. He was a tall man, well over six feet, and despite his age his long legs kept a lively pace. They walked around the edge of the pot field and onto a small path into the forest. The path stayed level for a time, then climbed to the top of a long sloping ridge that had been completely clear cut.

From their vantage point, Zoe saw tree-covered mountains roll away in every direction. In the west, gray fog from the Pacific Ocean drifted up the westward-facing drainages. The land seemed so vast and untamed by human hands, except overhead where the one sign of human existence marked the sky. A jet flying north scored the brilliant blue with its white contrail.

Zoe followed Sol into a steep valley, where the forest grew denser and darker. The trail shrank to little more than a deer path. Climbing back out would take a lot of energy. Would Clare be able to make it? Zoe guessed they'd already gone three miles, maybe four, considering how fast Sol was moving. No way Clare could hike at that speed.

They climbed down into even deeper shade, under trees that grew more massive, as if these were the original trees, dinosaur trees, from a time before civilization had altered the land. The air turned moist. Ferns and other lush, broad-leafed bushes grew all around. Finally, they reached the bottom, where a creek splashed playfully over rocks. Zoe heard laughter. Several women sat along the creek bank with their feet in the water.

"Hello, Rabbit and April," Sol greeted them and handed Rabbit the duffel bag. "I have to get back to the garden. Can you take Pele to her sister and give these supplies to Luna?"

"Yes, Sol." Rabbit took the bag.

Neither of the women had shoes, but they nimbly led Zoe barefoot a short way up the creek to where the forest widened into a clearing that was surrounded by enormous old-growth redwoods. A circle of women sat in the center, holding hands and singing a song Zoe didn't recognize. Clare wasn't there.

#

Jason watched Zoe follow Sol into the trees and called himself every kind of sap for the twinge of emotion he felt as he watched her go. He'd known her less than forty-eight hours, but he'd already slept with her twice. The thought made him grin. They'd been fully clothed, of course, but he'd enjoyed every moment. His last girlfriend had ditched him when he'd been promoted to undercover work. She hadn't liked him disappearing for days and weeks on end.

Zoe was nothing like he'd expected. She loved her sister, of course, but she continued to amaze him with her ability to adapt to new situations. The attack by Hanks, roughing it with no food or tent, her introduction to the grow and all the marijuana, she'd handled all of it remarkably well. He'd been particularly pleased when she'd refused to smoke the marijuana the Seekers had offered her. That showed a strength of character he admired.

"Come on, dude, fire up your chant." Fox clapped him on the shoulder as the men took their positions around the grow.

The deep, resonant sound of "Om" rose on the warm, sunny air, along with the pungent aroma of the marijuana. As Jason chanted and watched the plants sway gently in the light breeze, he remembered how good Zoe had felt in his arms, the fit perfect. His body responded.

Enough! he told himself. Time to take care of business.

He had to see if he could reach Porter. He looked up at the sun's position. It was almost time. He chanted and waited for the right moment to make his exit look natural. Like the other men who occasionally stepped into the trees to relieve themselves, he made his move. He entered the forest and headed for the location he'd identified that had decent satellite reception at certain times of the day, when the right satellite orbited overhead. He climbed quickly to the spot and removed the sat phone from its hiding place under a pile of rocks.

His boss answered immediately, "Parrish. Got your message."

"Hanks and his logger buddies burned down Harmony camp last night. They were apparently worried the Seekers' illegal activity would call attention to their own. The Seekers are now all at Sunrise Camp and the grow."

"What's that gotta do with Heller?"

"Unclear, but I heard Heller tell Sol he's going to do something with Derrick Hanks."

"I don't give a fuck about that logger. Any sign of the Feds? I heard through the grapevine they're getting ready to move."

"Not that I've seen, sir, but the crop's almost mature. The plants are budding out. The Seekers are talking about harvesting in the next week."

"Good. I'll get our team ready."

"Heller was at the grow yesterday."

"In person?"

"He met with Sol about Hanks. He's also become fixated on a young Seeker woman."

"Stay focused on Heller and the grow, Parrish. We need to nail him before the DEA moves in and steals our show."

#

Zoe followed Rabbit and April into the clearing. The circle of women sitting on the ground finished their song as they walked over to them.

"Welcome to our Retreat, Pele, I'm glad you came to join us." Luna smiled up at Zoe.

"I'm here for Clare. Where is she?" Zoe looked toward the tents that sat in the shadows under the towering redwoods.

"She's not there," Luna said, getting to her feet. "I'll take you to her."

Zoe followed Luna back to the creek. They walked a short distance upstream to where the stand of old-growth redwoods ended and the forest shrank in height. The sun sparkled on a bright pool of water and a small waterfall cascaded musically across a few small boulders. Clare sat in the sunshine on the sand beside the pool. Her eyes were closed and she was wrapped in a thick blanket. The sun lit up her blond hair like a halo. Despite her pale face, she looked peaceful.

Luna nodded toward Clare and then disappeared the way they'd come. Zoe walked over to her sister, who opened her eyes.

"You're hard to find!" Zoe said, taking a seat beside Clare on the sand. "I got to Sunrise Camp yesterday, but you'd already left."

"I'm so glad you're OK, Sis." Clare gave her a quick hug. "I was so worried when those men attacked Harmony."

"Me, too. Weren't you a sitting duck in the tent? How did you get away?"

"I crawled out the back of the tent. Sol was there. I wanted to go back for you, but he kept us all in a group. He told me you'd be safe because you were with Shadow."

"Really?" It surprised her that Sol had noticed her.

"Shadow is very careful and he takes care of people." Clare hitched the blanket higher around her shoulders and sighed heavily. "He was right to call you. From the first day he joined us, he noticed I wasn't as strong as the others. He's so kind. He does so many little things for me, like bringing me my food, and he always washes my dishes for me."

He must have been monitoring how much Clare ate. Zoe had done it herself when they were younger and

Clare wasn't feeling well. Hunger was a sign of health, the doctors had told her. No appetite indicated the opposite.

"He's a nice guy. Do you like him?" Zoe asked, wondering if her sister had a crush on Shadow.

"Not like that. He's too old for me. Besides, I have a boyfriend," Clare smiled.

"Who?" Zoe asked, surprised.

"Boon. He's gone to San Diego to bring back more Seekers for the harvest."

"Cool," Zoe said and then changed the topic, aware of the time passing. "Remember you said you'd come with me to see a doctor?"

"I don't know," Clare said. "Sol needs a lot of help now that it's almost harvest."

"He can't need that much help if all the Seeker women have come here. Besides, he said the harvest isn't for another week. The timing's perfect. Like I said before, come with me and I'll bring you back next weekend."

Clare was silent for a moment, thinking, and then nodded. "OK, but I want to talk to Sol first, just to make sure."

Zoe helped her sister to her feet and draped the blanket over Clare's shoulders. They walked back to the clearing where the circle of women sat with their eyes closed in quiet meditation around a large, rainbow-striped candle. Luna opened her eyes when they approached. She got up and stepped away from the circle to join them.

Zoe said, "Clare is coming with me. She needs to see a doctor."

Luna put her hands on Clare's shoulders and studied her face, as if searching for something.

"Is it OK?" Clare asked the older woman.

Luna frowned. "The full moon is tonight, my child. If you leave now, you will not benefit from the power that can be harnessed from its pure, healing energy. You will miss our full moon ritual."

Zoe spoke up, hoping to intervene before Luna convinced Clare to change her mind about leaving. "How about we check with Sol?"

Luna looked into Clare's face for a few seconds longer and then gave her a gentle hug. "Sol will know what you should do, Clarity. But you must understand," Luna said, looking at Zoe, "your Western medicine and authoritarian doctors won't restore your sister to health, because they are out of touch with the harmony of the universe and the powers that unite all living things."

Zoe clenched her teeth to bite back the retorts simmering inside her and then took a deep breath. Calmly, she said to Luna, "I'll bring her back soon."

The return trip to Sunrise Camp seemed to take forever. They made slow progress up the steep trail out of the cool canyon. The sun blasted down as they climbed onto the exposed ridgeline. The afternoon was swelteringly hot. Clare had to stop a lot and sit down to rest. They gave up having any sort of conversation, since it took most of Clare's energy just to plod up the trail. Zoe wished for the thousandth time that she had a clock so that she could check the time. She guessed the hike with Sol had taken less than an hour, but now... The sun was quickly sinking westward and Sunday was passing by too quickly. Her mind ran endlessly over the logistics of how they would get back to San Francisco without cash or a car. She still hadn't figured that out.

#

It was late afternoon when Jason spotted the two sisters coming out of the forest. Like the other Seeker men, he was still chanting at the grow, his voice raw from the effort. He waved at them. As they came over, he noticed how different they were. Zoe's face was flushed in the late afternoon sun, but Clarity's was white as marble. She looked exhausted.

"Where's Sol?" Zoe asked Jason, looking around for the Seeker leader. "Clare wants to talk to him before we leave."

"He's at Sunrise Camp. I'll come with you. It's almost dinnertime. You doing OK?" he asked Clarity as they followed the trail to the camp.

"Just tired," she said, her soft voice softer than usual.

Jason wondered how many more miles she could hike in her condition.

"Clare and I need to get to the City tonight," Zoe said. "Can we borrow the Seeker's van? I'll bring it back next weekend."

"You'll have to ask Sol about that," he said, doubting the Seekers could spare the van since Hanks had destroyed the other one.

"I could try giving Boon a call," Clarity spoke up.

"We need a phone to arrange any of these logistics, so the sooner we get to Woodsville, the better," Zoe said.

Jason nodded, liking her ability to think ahead. "I'll ask Sol to let me drive you down tonight."

They arrived at Sunrise Camp where a few Seeker men were preparing dinner. Sol sat talking with Bear by the fire ring, where a small fire burned. He stood up when he saw them and came over, his face filled with concern. He took Clarity's hands in his and studied her face.

"Your aura is fading," he said to her.

"That's why she needs to see a doctor," Zoe said, sounding impatient.

Jason spoke up, hoping to soothe the waters. "May I borrow the van to drive them to Woodsville?"

"I'm afraid that isn't possible." Sol shook his head and let go of Clarity's hands.

"What do you mean?" Zoe stepped around Jason.

"The van isn't here," Sol said.

"What?" Zoe stared at him.

"Fox took it."

"Where did he go?" Jason asked, wondering why Fox needed the van again.

"More folks are going to join us for the chant. He went to bring them," Sol said.

"When will he get back?" Zoe put her hands on her hips, frustration all over her face.

"Sometime later tonight. I'm sorry, but you just missed him."

"Damn it!" Zoe cursed.

"It's OK, Sis, we can go in the morning," Clarity said. "I'm going to lie down."

Zoe spun away. Jason followed her over to the fire, where she stood staring down into the licking flames.

"Even if Fox gets back soon, I don't think we can leave until the morning, not with Clare so tired," she said.

He could tell from her posture that Zoe felt defeated, despite her earlier angry outburst. She'd worked so hard to get there, and her sister had actually agreed to go with her to get medical help, which meant she'd succeeded in doing something he'd been unable to do. He wanted to put his arm around her and comfort her, but he was afraid the gesture might seem too familiar, especially with the other Seekers watching. Instead, he gently touched her arm and gave her an encouraging smile.

"Don't worry, I'll drive you to Woodsville first thing," he said.

FINDING CLARITY

***

CHAPTER EIGHT

Monday Morning, Sunrise Camp

The tent flap rustled and Shadow's voice called to Zoe from outside the tent. "Pele, I've got some bad news."

Zoe opened her eyes and realized she was alone. Her sister wasn't sleeping beside her in the small pup tent. She sat up and saw the outline of Shadow's body standing outside the tent, silhouetted against the bright morning light.

"Where's Clare?" Zoe asked.

"Gone."

"She's probably out using the bushes or something."

"No, she left with Sol. Bear just told me."

"What?" Zoe shoved off the blankets, all the warmth and comfort of sleep gone. She climbed out of the tent and yanked on her jacket. "She told me everything was a go last night."

"I thought so, too. Bear said they left really late last night, when Fox got back with the van."

Zoe's brain kicked into high gear, fired by the adrenaline and anger jolting through her body.

How could Clare take off? She was going to have to track her down, again. Again, damn it! Today was Monday and she was supposed to be at work.

"Where the hell did they go?" she asked as she walked with Shadow over to where the other Seeker men were eating oatmeal and sipping tea.

Shadow handed her a bowl of steaming oatmeal. "The black sand beach on the Lost Coast. Sol wants Clarity to try one more of his healing ceremonies, something about the 'Harvest Moon Ritual.'"

"She doesn't need another stupid ritual. She needs a doctor!" Zoe choked down a bite of the bland, undercooked oatmeal. "Why didn't she tell me she was leaving?"

Bear spoke up, "She checked in on you before they took off, but you were sacked out, Goddess Pele. She didn't have the heart to wake you up. Clarity's like that, you know, so kind and considerate."

"Isn't she?" But that wasn't what Zoe was thinking as she finished the oatmeal. Clare could be so damned irresponsible sometimes, driven by fleeting impulses of the moment rather than considering the big picture. Did her sister ever really think about how her actions affected others?

She put the empty bowl on the picnic table and turned to Shadow. "Where's that black sand beach?"

"A hell of a long way from here without wheels."

"I'd better get started."

"I'm coming with you."

"Don't you have to stay here and chant?"

"Probably, but you need me to find Clarity."

She wasn't about to argue. She had no idea which logging road led out of there or how to get to the black sand beach.

#

This trip to the Lost Coast was not part of his assignment, but he couldn't let Zoe go off on her own. She'd never find Clarity. On the up side, he'd be able to track Sol, plus he could check in with Charlie when they passed through Woodsville.

He watched Zoe move fluidly beside him down the steep road, her legs long and lithe, her body poised with the strength it took to maintain balance over the rough terrain.

"You're a great hiker," he said as she kept pace with him.

"I'm a runner," she said.

"Really?" He wanted to add that so was he, but Seekers were supposed to smoke pot and sit around contemplating their navels. He couldn't tell her the truth—that he ran for fun and as part of his training in physical readiness for his job.

"You're in pretty good shape, too," she said.

"Nothing like a vegan diet and working all day outdoors to stay buff." He picked up the pace to a jog.

They jogged on for a while, when Zoe spoke again. "The landscape here is so different than where I grew up in the desert."

Clarity had once mentioned where they were from, but Sol forbid the Seekers from talking about their personal histories. He believed it enslaved them and prevented them from exploring new ways of being.

Jason slowed the pace so they could talk without breathing too heavily. "I've never been to Arizona. What's it like?"

"Nothing like this, that's for sure. On clear days in the Sonoran desert, you can literally see for a hundred miles. There aren't any big trees or mountains to block your view."

"The mountains around here are still growing. They're part of an earthquake zone around the Pacific Ocean called the 'Ring of Fire' because of all the volcanoes." In school, he'd learned about the local geography, and he'd always loved the dramatic geology of the King Range.

"'Ring of Fire'? Sounds like the Johnny Cash song, though I don't know how desire fits in with all those earthquakes and volcanoes," Zoe laughed.

"I can, Pele," he grinned, glancing at her, but then quickly returned to a safer topic. "These mountains are in a constant battle against erosion. In fact, if it didn't rain so much, they'd be taller than Mount Everest."

"Really? Hard to believe it can rain so much! The desert is all about heat and the lack of rain."

Their backgrounds were so different. He found himself wanting to know more about her.

"When did you move to California?" he asked.

"Six months ago. I got a great job offer."

"Don't you miss your folks, moving so far away from them?"

She didn't immediately reply. He looked over and saw sadness and some deeper emotion cross her face.

"My parents are dead. It's just Clare and me now," she said.

Just the two of them alone in the world. Maybe that explained why she was so concerned about her sister.

"How about you?" Her question caught him off-guard.

"My parents passed away a while ago."

"You've got a sister, JoAnn, right? Any other brothers or sisters?"

"JoAnn lives in Garberville. I've got an older brother up in Eureka, too." He didn't add that Richard was a drunk like their dad had been. "My kid sister Tammy passed away."

"I'm sorry."

He was glad she didn't push for more details, because the pain had clenched like an iron fist in his chest as he remembered his sister.

Tammy and he had held down the family home after JoAnn got married and Richard moved to Eureka. Jason hadn't realized how lost Tammy had been when he'd moved to San Francisco to chase a job with the SFPD. He hadn't understood how much she needed his love and support. The guilt gnawed at him and added to the pain. The only relief he could muster was to remind himself that Heller would pay for taking advantage of Tammy, for using her up and destroying her.

"You grew up around here?" Zoe's voice distracted him from his dark thoughts.

"Over in Miranda. It's pretty similar to Woodsville. There used to be a lot of little logging towns up and down the Eel River. They thrived until they chopped down all the big trees. Now they survive on the money they make during tourist season, when folks come to Humboldt Redwoods State Park to see what's left of the original old-growth forests. We don't get many tourists, though. The economy's tough."

"What about all that pot you're growing?"

"The Seekers aren't about the money."

"That's pretty obvious from how you all are living, but the medical marijuana industry must be raking it in, what with all those pot clubs. I'm always seeing their ads in the local papers. Isn't there a push to make it completely legal?"

Just what the nation needs, a country of stoners, Jason scowled.

"You don't like the idea?" She'd caught his expression and looked at him curiously.

"Cannabis shouldn't be fun and games." He scrambled for his cover story. "The experience is so much more powerful and deep, so much more spiritual and healing than just getting a cheap thrill."

A cheap thrill that becomes less thrilling, a hunger for more excitement that grows, the need for stronger drugs, wilder thrills. It was all a one way ticket to hard drugs, as far as he was concerned. Though people claimed it had been disproven, he still believed marijuana was a gateway drug, especially based on what had happened with his sister.

"I smoked pot a few times in college, but it just made me paranoid and tired. Lord knows, I was always tired back then, and worried."

"About what?"

"Mainly about my sister and how I was going to pay for everything, especially her medical bills. I got a scholarship to Arizona State, but that just covered tuition, so I needed a job to cover the rest of our expenses, and for the medical insurance, too."

"You're a good sister."

"I try, but I wish Clare would face the reality about her health." She sounded exasperated. "I can't believe she just took off again."

"Sol can be very persuasive."

"Not to me," Zoe said emphatically.

You're no pushover. He liked that.

The dirt road flattened out as they reached the valley floor, and moments later, they reached the paved road.

"It's just a half mile to Woodsville, now," he said, as they struck out along the narrow gravel shoulder.

"What time do you think it is?"

He looked up at the sky. "Ten o'clock or so."

"It's Monday. I've gotta call work and let them know I won't be in today."

"What do you do?"

"Graphic design. I work at an advertising firm in the City. It's a great job and I love it, but I'm a newbie there. Low woman on the totem pole, so I haven't racked up any time off. I can't afford to lose my job, not now."

They walked onto the main street of Woodsville and a warm breeze kicked up, blowing from the south.

"How are we going to get to the black sand beach?" Zoe brushed her hair out of her face impatiently, tension obvious in the motion.

"Maybe we can borrow a car," he said as they approached the gas station and payphone.

"Who'd let us just borrow a car?"

"I'll check with Charlie at Logjammers, or maybe my brother-in-law Pete could loan us his truck. Make your calls. I'll be back in a jiffy."

No one was around, so Jason hurried across the street and went in Logjammers' front door. The place was empty, as he expected. Not even the most whiskey-soaked were in the bar on a Monday morning. He strode quickly across the barroom to the kitchen and then out back to the stockroom.

"Charlie?" he called.

"Hey, boyo." The aging bartender hoisted a case of beer in his arms.

"Let me." Jason grabbed the case and followed Charlie back into the bar.

"You want something to drink?" Charlie put two glasses on the bar and scooped ice into them. He filled one with water from the soda fountain.

Jason realized he was totally parched. "I'll have what you're having."

"Nothing like ice-cold water, far as I'm concerned." Charlie took a hearty swig from his glass. "Water is the secret of life."

Jason had no idea how old Charlie was, but he was easily over seventy, perhaps pushing eighty. Jason had never once seen him drink anything but water, not like his own dad, who used to drink whiskey like water. No wonder Charlie was still alive and his dad wasn't.

"That tastes great, especially after a long hike," Jason said.

Charlie eyed him perceptively. "A little early for a long hike. You want another sandwich?"

"You're a godsend, Charlie," Jason said, draining the glass, "but can you make it fast?"

"Sure thing."

They went into the kitchen, where Charlie began whipping up another of his monster subs.

"I've been keeping my eyes open like you said, boyo. Thought you might like to know Derrick Hanks came in here yesterday. He was full of fire and all worked up about the Seekers, but then Rob Heller showed up. Interesting thing. They sat together talking and drinking for several hours, at least Derrick was. Heller drank mostly green tea."

"What did they talk about?" Jason urged. He had no idea how long Zoe's phone call would take and he didn't want her walking in on them.

Charlie continued, "They made some kind of deal, something about Derrick driving his rig for Heller. It must've meant a good payout for Derrick, 'cause Heller kept buying him beers and Derrick was laughing and carrying on like there was no tomorrow." Charlie shook his head and clucked his tongue. "Blew my mind, seeing a logger hanging with the likes of Rob Heller. Only way that'd make sense is if Heller was promising Derrick the moon. Mark my words, no good will come of that, doing a deal with the devil."

Jason considered the information. Suddenly, the pieces fell into place. With the help of Hanks and his massive logging rig, Heller could get the entire harvest off the mountain in one trip. It would be way more efficient than relying on the Seekers and what was left of their derelict fleet.

Another, darker realization flashed through him. If Heller made peace with the loggers, there was nothing to stop him from using their rigs to transport the other drugs he was trafficking, too, including heroin and meth. In fact, if Heller played his cards right, the loggers wouldn't even know they were transporting more than just marijuana. He'd have to update Porter, but there wasn't time right now, not with Zoe waiting for him.

"Thanks for the info, Charlie. It's helpful," he said.

Charlie handed him the hefty sandwich and measured him with sharp blue eyes. "You still a cop, aren't you?"

When Jason shook his head, Charlie chuckled. "Don't worry. Your secret's safe with me."

He should've known that Charlie was too perceptive to buy his cover story, but though he trusted the old guy, he wasn't about to break cover.

"I hate to ask you for yet another favor, but I need to borrow some wheels."

"What for and how long?" Charlie asked, reaching under the counter. He held up a single key dangling from a shark-tooth chain.

"I've gotta help someone get out to the Lost Coast. We'll be back tonight. I promise," he added, when he saw the look of doubt on Charlie's face.

He just hoped he was telling the truth, but who knew how it was all going to play out.

#

Zoe sat shotgun in the bartender's pickup as Shadow got off the Redwood Highway at the town of Redway, which was bigger than Woodsville and had a school, a real grocery store, and a discount clothing store in addition to several bars, several gas stations with mini-marts, and a post office. He took a right and they drove west toward the ocean. She was relieved that they were finally on their way.

"How did it go with your company?" Shadow asked.

"OK, I guess," she shrugged. "I was able to reach our office manager. She told me I haven't earned any personal days yet, so I'm using up one of the two sick days I've accrued."

"You may need to use your last sick day, too. My brother-in-law Pete will probably loan you his truck to get back to the City, but if it gets too late tonight, we may have to wait until tomorrow to ask him."

"That's too much, asking your brother-in-law," Zoe shook her head. "If you could just give Clare and me a lift to Garberville, we can catch a bus from there. Of course, that's if we even find Clare today."

"Don't worry, we'll find her, and I'll talk to Pete. He won't mind you borrowing one of their cars." Shadow handed her a bulky package wrapped in white paper. "Charlie made us another one of these."

Zoe unwrapped an enormous submarine sandwich. The savory scents of peppers, deli meats, onion, and spreads filled the pickup's cabin.

"Mind if I start?" she asked, suddenly ravenous.

"Go ahead."

She needed two hands to hold the big sandwich together as she took a bite, and then another.

"Want some?" she asked, holding the sandwich toward Shadow.

"Sure," he said.

There was no way he could drive and hold such a big sandwich at the same time. Leaning over, she held it with both hands in front of his mouth as he kept his hands on the steering wheel. She'd never looked closely at him in the bright light of day. Despite his beard, he had a strong chin, a nice mouth.

"This messy," she laughed as a piece of lettuce fell out of the sandwich and onto his lap. A bit of mustard had caught in his beard, too. "You need a napkin."

"You want to clean me up?" His eyes met hers.

Her heart skipped a beat. Things were getting too intimate.

"I've kind of got my hands full right now." She nodded at the sandwich and then changed the subject. "Nice of the bartender to loan you his truck and give you more food."

"Charlie was like a grandpa to me when I was growing up."

She got the feeling there was more to the story, but Shadow didn't elaborate. She watched him devour the meat-filled sandwich, despite the Seekers' vegan doctrine, and wondered again about the odd contradictions between his behavior and who he claimed to be.

Like earlier, when he'd jogged with her down the road to Woodsville. It was obvious he enjoyed moving fast, just like she did, but the image of him as a long-haired, bearded hippie throwing off his tie-dye T-shirt, cargo pants, and hiking boots, and donning nylon shorts and running shoes to go out jogging just didn't seem right.

She looked out the passenger-side window after they finished the sandwich. The warm, moist air streamed in through the open window and blew across her face. It felt like she was in another country. The landscape was so rural and picturesque, so very different from the Arizona desert and urban San Francisco.

Their progress was slow as the small paved road wound its way past a few scattered farms, through occasional dense forests, and along narrow creeks. After a while, the road began to climb, switchbacking up the long, steep flanks of a huge mountain range.

"This is the King Range I told you about," Shadow said. "The mountains drop straight into the ocean. The shoreline is so extreme that no one can build a road along it."

"Doesn't sound like it has much of a coastline. Is that why it's called the 'Lost Coast'?"

"Actually, it's the one stretch of California coast where the Pacific Coast Highway doesn't go, so it's very remote."

They crested over a sharp, high pass. On the other side, the mountains arced steeply downward. Zoe braced herself against the dashboard as Shadow downshifted the truck to first gear. The transmission whined loudly. The sun winked through the trees to the west. Zoe thought about where they were heading.

"You've been to the Lost Coast before, right?" she asked.

"Not since I was kid. It's not an easy drive, as you can see, but our family made the trip to Shelter Cove a few times."

"Shelter Cove?"

"It's a tiny strip of land above the ocean, just a few vacation homes, an airstrip, a dry goods store. We camped out on the black sand beach once. I'll never forget it."

They passed a few hardscrabble houses that clung to notches carved out of the steep mountains, and then, abruptly, the forest stopped. Below them, the Pacific Ocean swept out and away into the distance, where it disappeared into a bank of fog that sat on the horizon, glowing in the late afternoon sun.

When they reached the small community of Shelter Cove, they headed north and drove to the trailhead parking for the Lost Coast Trail. The lot was only half full, with an assortment of cars, trucks, and RVs. The Seekers' van stood out like a beacon with its wild rainbow paint job and huge rust splotches. Zoe scanned the area, looking for her sister, but there was no one was around.

They climbed out of the truck and she inhaled the tangy marine air. She followed Shadow past a large signboard with a map and details about the trail.

"You can hike from one end of the Lost Coast to the other," he said as they followed a sandy path that led downhill between boulders to the beach. "It's twenty-five miles, point to point. I've always wanted to do the hike. It's a popular backpacking trip in the summer, but people have to time their hikes, because there are places where the trail gets covered by the ocean at high tide."

They reached the beach. Zoe stepped off the path and onto the black sand. She took in the spectacular view.

"This is amazing! I've never seen a black sand beach before."

The black sand beach ran north, bordered to the east by sheer walls of towering mountains and to the west by long breaking waves of turbulent surf. A strip of brilliant white foam ran the length of the beach where the waves washed onshore. The foam formed a vivid white line that contrasted starkly with the wet, black sand. A mist was starting to rise off the ocean as the sun sank into a cloudbank on the horizon. Unlike the windy beaches she was used to in the San Francisco, the air here was still.

She scanned the people on the beach. There weren't many, a few couples, a family with a dog.

"There's a group of people out there." Shadow pointed north across the long stretch of black sand beach.

Zoe peered through the rising mist. In the distance, she spotted the glow of a fire and the indistinct silhouettes of people around it.

"You think Clare's there?"

"Let's find out," he said, breaking into a jog.

She took off after him.

***

CHAPTER NINE

Monday Night, Lost Coast

Jason jogged with Zoe across the half-mile stretch of black sand beach toward the people gathered around the bonfire. The sun had set and night was coming fast. The bonfire blazed in the twilight. He scanned the group. It didn't take him long to identify the Seekers, once he noticed Sol's tall, thin figure and long white hair. The rhythmic beat of a drum and the sound of chanting voices grew more audible over the roar of the surf as he and Zoe approached.

"Looks like they've already begun the ritual," he said to her.

"Where's Clare?" she asked, increasing her speed.

He sprinted after her and grabbed her hand to slow her down. "Pele, stop."

She whirled and turned on him. "What do you think you're doing?"

"Getting you to stop for a moment and think. We need to come up with a plan before we approach Sol and your sister again."

"If she's not there, why do we need a plan?"

"She is there, lying on the sand. See?" He pointed to where Sol was bending over someone with long blond hair prone on the sand. It had to be Clarity.

"Think about it," he said, giving her hand a squeeze. "You managed to convince Clarity to leave with you last night, but then Sol persuaded her to change her mind. Whether it was intentional or not, he got her to side against you. If we barge into their ritual making demands, we may push her closer to him."

That seemed to get through to her. She unballed her fist and he let her hand go.

"What do you propose?"

"Keep a cool head and be patient. Sol doesn't respond well to demands. You've already seen that, so first let's go over and see what's going on. Depending on how your sister's doing and how the situation plays out, we can decide at that point the best course of action."

She shrugged. "Not much of a plan, but I guess it's better than going over there and trying to drag her away."

Though she had a temper, he liked that she wasn't stubborn.

They walked the rest of the way to the Seekers. The bonfire was ringed by a semicircle of redwood logs. Two other Seeker men were there with Sol, each seated on a log. One played a drum and the other chanted, while Sol stood, holding something smoking in his hand that he waved over Clarity's body.

"Hey there," Jason said, when they came within hailing distance.

"Shadow, Pele, welcome." Sol beckoned them into the semicircle of logs.

The chanter, whom Jason recognized as a Seeker named Jay stopped chanting. The other guy, a massive guy Sol had named Mountain continued to tap the large drum sitting on the ground between his knees in rhythmic intervals.

Clarity lay at Sol's feet on the sand near the fire, her eyes closed, and a serene expression on her face. A blanket was draped over her body. Even from ten feet back, Jason could feel the heat from the bonfire, so she had to be plenty warm.

Sol came over to them, his eyes fixated on Zoe, but she only had eyes for her sister. Jason could tell she wanted to rush to her sister's side and make sure Clarity was OK, but Zoe stayed where she was, her hands balled again into fists.

"Pele, you are most welcome here." Sol placed his hands on her shoulders.

She flinched, her eyes flying to Sol's, but Jason had to give her kudos for not jerking away from Sol. She'd taken what he'd said to heart about not alienating Sol.

"Your fire energy is powerful, Pele, as well as the love you harbor for your sister." Sol's hands stayed on her shoulders as he stared into her eyes. "Your presence will greatly strengthen the power of Clarity's lunar cleanse. Will you help us?"

"Lunar what?" Zoe looked back to her sister lying on the sand.

"The harvest moon contains the vital and nourishing moon energy that will heal Clarity. When we have completed the lunar cleanse, she will be healed."

Zoe shot a glance at Jason. She was probably thinking what he was, that the whole thing sounded loony, but he nodded for her to go ahead. They could talk to Clarity when the ritual was over.

"OK," Zoe shrugged.

Sol smiled broadly at her. "Your energy is wonderful."

He released her shoulders and went to pick up a bong sitting on the sand by one of the logs. He brought it back to them.

"Come, partake of Stellar Beauty." He held the bong to Zoe.

"'Stellar Beauty'?" she asked.

"A special strain of cannabis for moon rituals," Sol said, gesturing for her to take the bong.

She glanced at Jason again.

"It's OK. Sol knows what he's doing." Jason didn't buy Sol's hocus-pocus, but as Shadow he had to pretend to believe.

Sol held a match to the bong's bowl. "Inhale, Pele."

Zoe did as he said and started coughing violently. Sol handed the bong to Jason. He took a small hit. Immediately, the night seemed to sparkle, the light from the fire brighter, the sound of the drumming and the ocean louder. Euphoria swelled in his chest and he inhaled deeply. This wasn't ordinary marijuana. Had it been laced with something else?

Sol put the bong back on the ground and then pointed to the east and the white glow above the black mountainous ridge. "Behold, the harvest moon approaches!"

He rooted around inside a pack lying on the sand and pulled out two squat candles. He handed Zoe a red one and Jason a green one that smelled like green apples. He had them hold the candles with both hands and stand outside the semicircle of the logs. He positioned Jason on the north side and Zoe on the south. He had Jay, who was holding a blue candle, stand on the west side, closest to the ocean. Sol walked around the outside of the logs to the open side of the semicircle that faced east. Clarity lay on that side by the fire. He placed a yellow candle on the sand outside the circle on that side and then took a flaming poker and lit the candle.

"This is the East and our point of preference tonight." He turned, facing east, and spread his arms wide.

The moon's full disc began to emerge over the ridge, a brilliant white presence that lit up the sky.

Sol shouted, "We call to the East, to the powers of the rising moon, the rising of the light. We welcome you to our circle and ask that you bring possibility. May your light guide Clarity and all of us to a place of hope and healing."

Picking up the poker again, he relit it in the bonfire, and then moved around the outside of the semicircle of logs to Jason. He lit the green candle in Jason's hands, stuck the poker in the sand, and then opened his arms to the north, shouting, "We call to the North, to the powers of the earth, the solid and the strong, we welcome you."

He repeated the same action with Jay shouting, "We call to the West, to the powers of the waters, the clear and the cleansing, we welcome you."

When Sol got to Zoe, he said, "We call to the South, to the powers of fire, the fuel and energy of will, we welcome you."

He stepped back inside the logs and threw the poker on the fire. He picked up the still-smoking sage bundle, held it to the bonfire's flames to reignite it, and then slowly walked the compass points made by the circle of four burning candles.

"Let this purify our sacred space." He waved the burning sage around in the air over his head, keeping time with Mountain's rhythmic drumming.

When he reached Clarity, he stopped and lowered the smoking sage to hold it several feet above her. He slowly wafted it along the length of her prone body.

"May this protect you and may it help heal you, body and soul."

Clarity continued to lie still with her eyes closed. Her pale white skin and her long blond hair lay about her, giving Jason the disturbing impression that she'd died. He looked over at Zoe, who was staring at her sister. Was she thinking the same thing?

#

Was she too late? Zoe stared at her sister lying in the sand. Had Clare's kidney function collapsed and made her slip into a coma?

Zoe wanted to rush over and rouse her, get her to move or at least open her eyes, something to reassure her that Clare was OK. She could tell the pot was intensifying her fear and concern, as well as all her senses.

She bit her lip so hard she tasted blood and forced herself to stay where she was and obey Sol. The red candle in her hands felt warm in the cool night and smelled of cinnamon, its spicy, sweet scent mixing with the odor of the burning sage, the wood smoke, and the salty ocean.

The huge guy sitting on the log across from her kept up a rhythm on the big drum as the full moon rose, large and luminous over the tree-covered ridge. It flooded the black sand beach and the surf with eerie light. The moonlight felt cold and white on her face.

Sol leaned over Clare and glided the smoking sage slowly above her body from her head to her toes and then back again, repeating the motion as he began to chant something Zoe couldn't hear over the sound of the drumming.

A sudden breeze kicked up, magnifying the pungent scents of the sage smoke and wood fire and mixing them with the cinnamon scent of her candle. It sent the campfire flames dancing and flaring upward. The breeze moved across her face, and though she could feel it in her hair, her own candle flame didn't waver. Its own flame stayed strangely steady, its little warmth strong against the cool breeze.

Something weird was going on—or was it because she was high?

The big Seeker beat the drum faster and the breeze increased. Zoe looked over at Shadow's green candle and then the other guy's blue one. Despite the fact the breeze was quickly growing into a spiraling wind that seemed to spin in whorls around them, neither of their flames wavered, either.

The drumming reached a fever pitch, a pounding, pulsing rhythm that overpowered all other sounds, even the roar of the surf.

Suddenly, Clare sat up. She grabbed the sage bundle from Sol, who stepped back from her. She held the smoking sage high above her head, like an offering, her eyes open and focused on the full moon. The drummer stopped drumming. Just as abruptly, the wind stopped.

It felt like they were waiting for something. The moment stretched longer and longer. Zoe had no idea how much time passed, but she felt like she was holding her breath. She kept her eyes on her sister.

Clare's sage offering crackled, flared to life, and burst into a flaming torch of light, a vivid beacon in the night. Just as suddenly, Clare cried out, a high-pitched shrieking wail. She threw the offering into the fire. The action seemed to take everything out of her, and she collapsed back onto the sand and lay unmoving.

Fear gripped Zoe and she started to go to her, but Sol stopped her with a firm hand on her arm.

"Wait," he whispered.

Zoe's candle suddenly spluttered out, despite the lack of wind. She glanced at Shadow. His candle had gone out, too, and so had the other guy's.

The full moon had climbed higher above the horizon. It was so bright it cast shadows on the beach, almost as if it were daylight. There were no stars in its silvery sheen. A dark shape was coming, soaring down from the mountain ridge in the east.

Zoe held her breath as the thing drew closer, like an arrow coming straight at them. It was a pure white owl, enormous and silent, gliding on unmoving wings. It flew directly over the group and then circled the fire, its flat face and unblinking yellow eyes turned to Clare, where she lay on the sand beside the fire.

Uttering a piercing cry, it circled Clare three times and then rose on the warm updraft from the fire. It flew toward the moon and seemed to disappear into the blinding white orb.

For a stunned moment, they all stood frozen. Then, Clare opened her eyes and pushed herself up into a sitting position. Zoe rushed over and dropped to her knees beside her.

"Are you OK?" She took Clare's hands in hers. There was something about the physical sensation of holding

Clare's hands that instantly reassured her, despite the fact that they were ice cold.

"Oh yes. I feel wonderful." Clare looked up at the moon and then smiled at Zoe. She let go of Zoe's hands and stood up. "I need to thank Sol for healing me."

"What?" Zoe scrambled to her feet, planning to follow Clare to where Sol was stowing the ritual items in his pack, but Shadow stepped in front of her and blocked her way.

"Give her a minute," he said quietly.

Zoe looked past him and watched Sol's long arms wrap around Clare in a fatherly embrace. The sight pissed her off. The cult leader was using his persuasive powers to keep Clare from getting the medical help she needed, appealing to Clare's longing for a dad.

"No way that ritual magically cured her kidneys. She's in total denial!" she whispered furiously to Shadow.

"You're not going to get anywhere with her if you launch a full-frontal assault."

He had a point. She scowled and tried to think of another way to talk some sense into Clare. She'd always found the direct approach to be the right approach, but the pot was messing with her thinking, and she couldn't think of how to convince her sister that Sol wasn't her savior.

Sol released Clare and slung the backpack over his shoulders. Then, he addressed the group. "Friends, tonight we have witnessed powerful magic. The night eagle's visitation brings the promise of transition and transformation to Clarity. Our work is done here. Let us go."

He turned and started back across the black sand beach with Clarity at his side. Zoe watched them leave in disbelief. Clare couldn't stay living in the middle of the remote forest, not with the risk of kidney failure. If she went into a coma, would Sol recognize the danger, or would he think it was some "spiritual state" and do nothing?

It was now or never. Zoe pushed past Shadow and rushed after her sister.

#

Jason trailed Zoe and her sister across the black sand beach, listening to them argue. He had to give Zoe credit for trying with all her might to convince Clarity to come back with her to San Francisco, but by the time they reached the vehicles, it was clear that Clarity couldn't be swayed. She was adamantly convinced that Sol had cured her. Sol wasn't helping.

"I urge you to come back with us to Sunrise Camp," Sol said to Zoe as he placed his backpack in the back of the Seekers' van. "Your energy tonight was instrumental in bringing the night eagle. It made the harvest moon ritual a success for Clarity. Please, let us show our appreciation and come with us. Your fire energy will help our garden grow."

Zoe turned her frustration on Sol. "Are you kidding me? Clare's not healed! And there's no way in hell I'll help you with your damned garden!"

Jason tuned out the dispute raging between Zoe and Sol and looked around the parking lot. Clarity sat on a boulder overlooking the beach and ocean. The other two Seeker men sat inside the van, smoking a joint. The parking lot had seemed deserted when they'd first climbed up from the beach, but now, he sensed someone watching them. He looked across the moonlit space to the far side, where a tall stand of pine trees cast deep shadows. He narrowed his eyes and peered into the darkness. In the shadows under the trees, he saw the unmistakable hulking form of a black Hummer. Heller.

Zoe tugged on his arm and broke his concentration. He looked down at her.

"Can you give me a ride?" she said, her face bright in the moonlight.

"What?" He'd missed the rest of her argument with Sol.

"Clare won't go, so I give up."

"Really?" He couldn't believe she'd given up.

She didn't answer his question. Instead, she said, "Could you give me a lift to Garberville? There's got to be a bus or something from there to San Francisco. I need to get back to work."

"Sure," he said, but then a flash across the parking lot caught his eye.

He looked up, just in time to see Clarity's blond head disappear into the black Hummer.

#

"Damn it!" Shadow cursed and took off past Zoe. He ran full speed away from her.

What was wrong?

A powerful engine fired up at the far end of the parking lot. Shadow sprinted after a giant black Hummer that roared out onto the road.

Zoe looked around. Sol was standing on the far side of the van, talking to the driver, but where was her sister? Clare had been on a rock looking at the view in the moonlight, but now she'd disappeared.

Zoe ran after Shadow out of the parking lot, racing to catch up with him. The Hummer's taillights disappeared around a bend in the road just as she reached Shadow, who stood with his hands on his knees, bent over, and breathing heavily.

"Brock's taken Clarity," he gasped.

"What?"

"Come on!" Shadow spun around and dashed back to the parking lot.

Zoe ran after him to the pickup truck. No sooner had she swung her door closed, then Shadow threw the truck into reverse and stomped on the accelerator. They peeled out of the parking lot, burning rubber.

"I don't understand. Why would he do that?" She braced herself against the pickup's metal frame as the truck lurched wildly around a corner. She hadn't even seen Brock at the parking lot.

Shadow didn't answer. She could tell he was pushing the limits of what the truck could handle as they hurtled around the tight switchbacks and hairpin turns of the road as it climbed swiftly away from the ocean.

"There's only one way out of here, so they've gotta be on this road," Shadow muttered, as if talking to himself.

"What's the rush?" Zoe asked as the truck veered wide on a tight corner. She prayed it was late enough in the evening that they wouldn't meet any oncoming cars on the narrow, undivided road.

Shadow muscled the truck back onto their side of the road. In the reflected glow of the headlights, his face looked grim and his jaw clenched through his beard.

"We have to catch them." He said nothing more.

What wasn't he telling her?

"You obviously know what's going on, so give me some answers!" she demanded.

He shot her a tortured look. "I've known Rob Heller since we were kids. The guy's bad news."

Zoe thought about the man Sol had named Brock. She remembered him showing up at the pot field, and earlier, when he'd tried to hit on her at the Woodsville bar. He certainly didn't seem to fit with the Seekers, not with his bald head and clean-shaven face, or his expensive clothes. Despite being a bit creepy, he seemed a step up from the practically homeless, pot-obsessed Seekers. Was he the bad man Shadow had first warned her about? Clare had denied any bad men around the Seekers, but Zoe was well-aware of her denial issues.

"'Bad news'? What does that mean? Did he kill someone or something?"

"He's guilty of at least one murder."

"Wasn't he convicted?"

"No. They ruled it an accidental overdose."

"From pot?"

"Heroin."

"I don't get it. What does that have to do with Clare?"

"God, I should have seen this coming!" Shadow slammed the steering wheel hard with the flat of his hand, and fear skittered through Zoe.

"What do you mean?" She stared at him.

The reflected glow of the headlights cast his face in stark shadows. As if he felt her studying him, he looked across at her. His eyes were dark with a complex mix of rage, frustration, and despair.

"He killed my sister," he said.

#

Jason gripped the steering wheel in a death grip as the pickup bounced over the poorly paved road. The moment he'd ID'd Heller in the parking lot, he should've realized Heller was there for Clarity.

Damn it!

"He killed your sister?"

He felt Zoe staring at him. He wasn't sure how much he could open up to her about Tammy. It was all still too raw. He'd only broached the subject once before, at the funeral, when he'd talked to JoAnn. She'd tried to tell him it wasn't his fault, that Tammy had voluntarily gotten into the relationship with Heller and that her OD was her own fault. He knew better. He'd gone off to San Francisco and left Tammy, just when she needed him most.

"Your sister OD'd?" Zoe's voice broke into his thoughts.

"That was the official finding, but I know what really happened, even if they couldn't find the forensic evidence to prove it."

Tammy had been found naked and alone, submerged in a motel bathtub with a needle in her arm, the place wiped free of any fingerprints but her own. The police had considered it an open and shut case, another sad ending to a heroin junkie, but Jason knew the truth. Heller had a done a bang-up job covering his tracks.

"What really happened?" Zoe asked.

"Tammy was my kid sister by seven years. She'd just graduated from college in New York City and had come home for a spell. Maybe she was bored after living in New York. Brock's a big shot around here, so maybe she was flattered when he came sniffing around. She was ripe for the picking, and I was—"

Too busy chasing my career, he thought, and steeled himself against remembering what he'd found in Heller's barn that the night after Tammy died, when he'd gone snooping and looking for answers.

He didn't want to scare Zoe, so all he said was, "We have to get Clarity away from Brock, the sooner, the better."

"Let's call the cops."

"Too risky. Brock will hear their sirens blaring a mile away. Plenty of time for him to hide Clarity—"

—or worse, but he left the words unsaid.

"Do you have a plan?" Zoe asked.

"We'll think of something."

They drove into Redway. The town was dark at that late hour. Still no sign of the Hummer. Heller must drive like a bat of hell. They reached the Redwood Highway and Jason pulled to a stop. The truck engine idled. Frustration overtook him.

"What's up?" Zoe sounded uncharacteristically scared.

"Considering our options." He reached out and took her hand. The reassuring squeeze he gave her helped him feel a little better, too.

"Where could they have gone?" she asked.

"Most likely to his compound." He looked at the clock on the dashboard. It was after midnight.

"OK, so let's go!" Zoe said.

"We can't, not tonight."

"But what about Clare? From what you just said about your sister, she's in terrible danger!" Zoe pushed his hand away.

"I'm sorry, but we don't have a choice." He rubbed his eyes, thinking. "We can't go after her without help, and not without scoping the place out first. He may have guards, and he's definitely got guns. We need a place to crash and plan strategy."

Zoe said nothing, but it was obvious in the tense silence that she was unhappy about the situation. He put the truck in gear and headed southbound on the highway to Garberville.

"Where are we going?" she asked.

"My sister JoAnn's. She lives near Garberville."

"This late? Won't we wake her up?"

"We won't have to. I've got a key." He just hoped JoAnn didn't have other visitors.

Except for a few long-haul trucks, the highway was devoid of traffic. The drive to Garberville didn't take long. His sister lived just outside of town in a rural area. He pulled into the driveway and around to one of the small outbuildings. A motion sensor light clicked on.

"JoAnn won't mind if we stay here?" Zoe asked as he unlocked the door. She was looking back toward the main house, where the two-story place was dark.

"No, my brother-in-law Pete built this place for visitors. I've crashed here a few times."

They entered the tiny main room that had a kitchenette on one side and a couch and coffee table on the other. He checked the two small bedrooms and the bathroom. Good, no surprises.

He turned back to Zoe. "Each bedroom has a double, so your choice."

She looked as tired as he felt, and he had the urge to cuddle her to sleep in one of the beds.

"Real beds and a bathroom, what luxury!" she said, heading for the bathroom.

He checked the kitchenette for food and found a loaf of bread in the freezer and some peanut butter and huckleberry jam in the refrigerator. There was nothing to drink but water. He made two sandwiches and put them on the coffee table along with two glasses of water.

"This doesn't exactly qualify as dinner, but you want a PB&J?" he said when she came back.

"Yes, please." She took a bite and looked up. "What kind of jam is this? It's delicious."

"Native huckleberry. It grows like a weed around the back of this place. JoAnn picks the berries and makes jam in September. We're lucky to get some." His sandwich tasted fantastic.

The adrenaline of the chase was wearing off, leaving him suddenly ravenously hungry. Hunger had a way of doing that, of ratcheting up his senses. It focused and intensified his need, such that the act of satiation became pure bliss. He watched her finish her sandwich. The way she moved her mouth made him want to kiss her. Instead, he gathered the plates.

"I'll wash these. Why don't you go to bed?" he said.

"I don't know if I can." She picked up a kitchen towel and dried the plates as he washed them. "I hate it that there's nothing we can do right now. It just doesn't feel right, being here safe and sound and simply going to bed while Clare's out there somewhere, in danger."

She looked so frustrated and scared and tired, he had to hold her. He put his arms around her and savored the feel of her against him. Her curly hair teased his face and smelled of mountains and mist and ocean. She sighed and relaxed as he tucked her more closely to him.

"The best thing we can do is go to bed. We'll need clear heads in the morning," he said, releasing her.

He congratulated himself for sounding so logical and neutral, when his body wanted nothing more than to crawl into bed with her. It was going to be a long, short night.

***

CHAPTER TEN

Tuesday Morning, Garberville

Zoe jolted awake to a strange sound, a kind of low-level hum. She lay motionless on the bed, which felt soft and squishy after roughing it the last few nights. She realized the sound came from the refrigerator in Shadow's sister's guest house. Normally, she wouldn't have noticed it, but after spending so much time in the silent redwoods, the sound seemed alien and unfamiliar.

Light seeped through the blinds. She rolled over and looked at the digital clock on the bedside table. It was good to be back in civilization again, where people kept track of the time. Seven o'clock. Ten hours had gone by since Clare had disappeared with Brock.

God, I hope she's OK, she thought as she hurried out of bed and pulled on her clothes.

She checked the place for Shadow. The main room was empty, and though the sheets and blankets were rumpled in the other bedroom, there was no sign of him. Maybe he'd gone to see his sister. She went into the bathroom. It was fully supplied with towels, soap and shampoo. Despite feeling pressed for time, she was desperate for a quick shower after four days of roughing it. She stripped and hurried into the blissfully warm water.

Last night, she'd sunk into a pretty low place, but as the water streamed over her, washing away the dirt and grime, she determined that today was going to be a new day. Things were going to go better. Shadow and she would get her sister and then they'd get back to San Francisco.

Minutes later, she hurried out of the guest house, feeling more like herself. It was a beautiful morning. The sun shone through the trees and across the open area of the property. She looked around, but there was no sign of Charlie's pickup truck.

She crossed the driveway to the aging two-story main house, its sky-blue paint starting to peel, and rang the doorbell. Somewhere inside, footsteps pounded, and excited children's voices called out. A minute later, the front door was opened by a dark-haired woman in a uniform with a gas company logo. A little girl and boy looked curiously up at Zoe.

"You must be Pele. I'm JoAnn, Jason's sister." JoAnn didn't use his Seeker name and she didn't smile at Zoe. Her eyes traveled over Zoe from head to toe, her mouth a firm line, her expression unreadable.

Zoe got the impression that JoAnn didn't care for the Seekers, judging by her restrained manner.

Zoe responded politely, "Nice to meet you. My name's actually Zoe, Zoe Thompson."

"This is Cindy and David." JoAnn looked down at her children. "Say 'hi' to Zoe."

"Hi Zoe, we're gonna have blueberry muffins, yummy!" Cindy crowed and ran down the hall, her younger brother on her heels.

"Is Shadow here?" Zoe asked.

"He went with my husband to return Charlie's truck. They should be back soon. We're about to have breakfast," JoAnn said and turned back inside.

Zoe followed her to the kitchen, which was filled with the delicious smells of coffee, bacon and eggs, and fresh muffins in the oven. The sun streamed in the big eastern window and the room was bright and cheery. The kids sat bouncing on their seats, eagerly waiting for their breakfast at the kitchen table as JoAnn bustled about getting everything ready. Zoe stayed standing, feeling awkward for intruding.

"Thanks for letting me crash your breakfast," she said. "Shadow told me it was OK if we stayed at your guest house last night. I hope he was right?"

"Anything for family," JoAnn said. She slid a tray of perfectly plumped blueberry muffins from the oven and then went to set the table.

Zoe was thankful JoAnn didn't make small talk or ask pointed questions about why she was there. Talking about Clare and Brock might remind JoAnn of Tammy, and Zoe didn't want to make the situation any more awkward than it already felt.

She went over to the coffeemaker on the counter. "Mind if I have a cup?"

"Help yourself." JoAnn handed her a mug from the cupboard.

"Thanks." Zoe poured herself a cup of coffee while JoAnn served breakfast to the kids. She took a sip. It was deliciously strong and hot.

The outside kitchen door creaked open and a man wearing a ranger uniform stepped inside.

"Daddy!" Cindy shouted and launched out of her seat and into her dad's arms.

"Good morning, sweetie." Pete hugged his daughter.

Shadow followed Pete and smiled when he saw her. He headed over to where she stood at the counter with her coffee.

"Glad to see you're up," he said quietly.

She followed him to the kitchen table and sat down.

"Great-looking spread, JoAnn," Shadow said to his sister as she dished out the food.

JoAnn nodded, her green eyes so like her brother's as she looked at Zoe and then at Shadow, before taking a seat at the table.

Zoe shoveled a forkful of eggs into her mouth, aware that JoAnn and Pete were watching the two of them together. It was obvious they thought she and Shadow were a couple. The little kids chattered happily with each other, while the adults ate quickly and silently. Zoe noticed Shadow devoured his bacon and eggs.

Again, he didn't seem to care that he was violating Seeker philosophy, or maybe he just couldn't resist his sister's cooking. The food was prepared to perfection.

A big red kitchen clock on the wall caught Zoe's eye. It read eight o'clock. Eleven hours since Brock took Clare.

JoAnn jumped to her feet. "Sorry to dine and dash, but come on kids, we've gotta get you to school so I can go to work."

She gathered Cindy and David's plates along with her own and put them in the sink. She gave her husband a peck on the cheek and then shot a quick glance at Shadow before she hurried out after the kids.

Pete pushed back from the table and went to pour himself a cup of coffee in a travel mug.

"We'll clean up," Shadow said to his brother-in-law.

Pete gave him a stern look. "I don't know what you're playing at with those Seekers, Jason, and I don't want to know, but things always get crazy around here at harvest time. You be careful, OK?"

"Always, Pete. Thanks again for everything," Shadow said, but Pete was already headed out the door.

Shadow went to the sink to wash the dishes. Zoe picked up a dishtowel and started drying.

"They're kind of conservative, aren't they?" she asked.

Shadow nodded and handed her a plate. "Definitely straight shooters. I've tried to explain Sol's philosophy to them, but they think I'm nuts. As far as they're concerned, the Seekers are a bunch of cannabis-crazed hippies."

"Did you tell them I'm a Seeker, too?"

"What makes you say that?"

"JoAnn called me Pele when we first met, and she didn't exactly lay out the welcome mat."

"She's just being protective. She and Pete, they're good people, salt of the earth."

"Did you tell them about Clare?"

"No, but I talked some with Pete. He's loaning us his truck and says we can use their guest house again if we need it. He also told me something very interesting."

"Yes?" Zoe took the last pan from Shadow to dry.

"He told me there's a group of Seekers camped at the local campground. We need to talk to them, because we're going to need help getting Clarity away from Brock."

Worry flooded through her again as she thought of Clare with Brock and what Shadow had told her about his kid sister. "You think she's OK?"

"She will be, when we get her out of there," he said.

She looked at the kitchen clock again and suddenly remembered that it was Tuesday. She had to call work.

"Before we go, I've got to call my company and let them know I'm still MIA. Do you think JoAnn and Pete would mind if I use their phone to make a long distance call?"

"No, but we've gotta get going."

"I know, but I can't afford to lose my job, either. Just give me a few minutes, OK?"

"I'll grab a shower and be back in five. Phone's over there." He pointed to the small desk tucked away at the far end of the kitchen.

#

Jason glanced at Zoe as they drove to the campground outside of Garberville. Her dark red hair blew in the breeze coming through the open window.

"My boss has given me the rest of the week off," she said, pushing her hair out of her eyes. "I'll owe major overtime, but at least I'll still have a job. What a relief!"

"Great!" He loved that she was so responsible.

Loved? The word stopped him short.

He was on assignment. She was just one of the people along the way. As soon as they rescued Clarity, she'd be back to San Francisco and he'd probably never see her again. The thought bummed him out.

"So what's the plan?" She turned on the truck's bench seat to look at him.

"First, let's see if the Seekers can help us. Then, we need to find out if Brock took Clarity to his compound."

They pulled into the Garberville campground. Less than half the campsites were occupied, predominantly by RVs and retirees. Jason drove around the twists and turns of the one-way road to the back of the place, which pushed into a stand of second-growth redwoods at the mouth of a creek. At the farthest campsite were a cluster of ramshackle tents and tarps. Jason parked the pickup beside an ancient VW bus. A dusty station wagon was parked on the far side.

They got out and walked over to a group of people at the campsite's picnic table. A couple of young women and a young man sat at the table, and four other guys stood around it, finishing their breakfast. One woman attempted to hide a bong under the table, but her attempt was foiled by the marijuana smoke floating in the still morning air.

Jason recognized one of the guys standing beside the table. It was Clarity's boyfriend, Boon, who'd left Harmony a week ago to gather more Seekers for the harvest.

"Long time no see!" He stepped forward and clapped Boon on the shoulder.

"Shadow, dude," Boon returned his greeting.

"What are you doing camping here?" Jason asked.

"Our stop in San Francisco took longer than expected. We didn't get into town until late last night, and I didn't want to drive to Harmony in the dark. It's way too easy to get lost on those dirt roads."

"Good thinking," Jason said. He liked Boon, who seemed more rational and competent than many of the airy-fairy Seekers. He might be the best one to help them rescue Clarity.

Boon introduced his friends and Jason introduced Zoe.

"You're Clarity's sister? I'm honored to meet you, Pele." Boon gave Zoe a little bow.

"Clare told me you two are together." Zoe looked Boon up and down.

"That's all she said?" Boon looked disappointed. "She's my heart and soul. I love her." He put his hand to his heart.

"Then why—" Zoe was interrupted by the young woman with the bong.

"Wanna wake and bake?" The woman put the bong on the picnic table, relaxed now that she knew Jason and Zoe weren't strangers. "This Humboldt stuff's primo."

"Not right now, thanks," Jason said and motioned for Zoe and Boon to follow him over to where the cars were parked and out of the earshot of the others.

"We need your help," he said quietly to Boon.

"What's going on?" Boon asked.

"I'm sorry, Boon, but Brock's taken Clarity. She's in danger and we need to get her back."

Boon's face registered confusion and he looked at Jason. "Why's she in danger from Brock? She's been trying to help him."

How could Boon and Clarity be so blind? Impatience surged through Jason and he struggled to find the right words to make Boon understand.

Zoe voice broke into his thoughts as she addressed Boon. "What do you mean about her trying to help him?"

"With meditation and spiritual healing, stuff like that. Sol has, too. Brock's got demons—"

"Maybe the situation's not as bad as you think, Shadow?" Zoe looked at him hopefully.

"Trust me, Brock's a very dangerous man," he said through clenched teeth and turned to Boon. "We have to get Clarity away from him, as soon as possible, and we need your help."

"OK." Boon didn't look convinced. He gestured toward the other Seekers at the campsite. "Those guys don't know the way to Harmony. Can I take drive them there, first?"

"Everyone's at Sunrise Camp and the garden now." Jason didn't waste time telling Boon about what had happened to Harmony. Boon was bound to find out soon enough. He continued, "Think you can be back in a couple of hours?"

"Sure, but I'd better start getting everyone motivated." Boon turned to walk back to the campsite.

"Meet us at Logjammers in Woodsville," Jason called after him.

Jason looked at Zoe. "Time to check out Brock's place."

They climbed into the pickup and headed north, away from Garberville toward Woodsville.

#

Shadow wasn't kidding when he said Brock had a big compound. They reached it several miles before Woodsville, where it bordered the right side of the road for a long stretch. Zoe didn't like what she saw. A double line of vicious-looking barbed wire ran along the top of the fence. Shadow hit the gas as they approached and then passed the entrance gate, but Zoe had enough time to see a keypad box and a security camera as they drove by.

"What are we going to do?" she asked, looking out the window at the forbidding fence that continued on the other side of the entrance gate.

"We're going to sneak onto his property."

"How? The place is a fortress."

"I've done it before."

"You have? When?"

"I'll tell you another time."

Zoe wanted to ask more questions, but Shadow wasn't paying attention as he slowed the truck and looked out her passenger-side window. They'd gone maybe a quarter mile past the entrance when the barbed wire fence ended.

"This is it," he said, braking the truck.

He pulled off the paved road onto a small dirt road that skirted the northern edge of Brock's compound. They drove along the single-lane dirt road until they were well out of sight of the paved road. When they reached a wide stretch, Shadow turned the truck around and pulled it as far as he could to the side of the road.

"Wait here. I'll be back shortly," he said, opening the driver-side door and turning to look at her.

"I'm coming, too." She swung open her door and started to get out.

Shadow reached across and grabbed her hand, stopping her. "Please, let me go and get the lay of the land first."

"And sit idly by? No way!" She shook off his grip and jumped out of the truck.

She heard him cursing under his breath, something about bossy women, as he headed around to the back of the pickup. She went to see what he was doing. He'd picked up some kind of tool.

"What's that?" she asked.

"Bolt cutters. Come on."

He set off into the trees toward Brock's property. She followed him on the barest of paths, weaving past prickly blackberry bushes and over occasional rocks. In a short time, they reached the barbed-wire fence and then turned onto what looked like an animal path that paralleled the fence line. She looked up apprehensively at the barbed wire fence. Brock obviously didn't want intruders. She followed Shadow past a spot where a hole in the fence had once been repaired and continued a few dozen feet farther.

"This'll work," he muttered, coming to a stop.

He crouched and used the bolt cutters to snip the wires of the fence.

"Did you make that hole back there?" she whispered, looking back along the fence line.

He nodded. "Keep your eyes and ears perked while I do this."

She looked around, her anxiety feeling at odds with the peaceful day. The sun shone almost directly overhead and the air was warm, smelling of dry earth and pine needles. A bird twittered in the trees nearby, but besides that and the quiet snipping sound of Shadow's work, the place was quiet. Inside the fence, she saw a dirt road that paralleled the fence line, and beyond that, more trees. There was no sign of any buildings or anything else. How on earth were they going to find Clare on such a big property?

She watched Shadow pull a section of the fence free, making a hole big enough for them to crawl through. Her misgivings increased as she followed him through the hole.

"How can we sneak around in broad daylight without getting caught?" she asked, watching him loosely fit the wire section back over the hole. She doubted Brock would be very happy if he caught them trespassing. With all that barbed wire, he definitely didn't want uninvited visitors.

"We can't wait until tonight. We're just lucky Brock hates dogs, otherwise what we're doing would be impossible." He started across the dirt road toward the trees on the far side.

If he'd meant to reassure her, he hadn't.

In the bright daylight, she felt like they were walking targets. She cringed as their feet crunched on the leaves and twigs under the trees. They'd gone less than a hundred feet when Shadow stopped and held up his hand. Zoe froze behind him. Cigarette smoke wafted toward them on the slight breeze. She sensed someone standing just ahead, beyond the last line of trees.

She looked at Shadow for guidance but did a double-take when she saw him. Gone was the casual, laid-back Seeker she knew, replaced by someone predatory. His whole body was tensed and alert, his eyes narrowed as he scanned the scene, as if he'd done this kind of surveillance before.

Because that's what it is, she realized. He was conducting surveillance of Brock's compound, like he was a spy or a cop. But if he'd been a police officer like her dad had been, would he have cut the fence and trespassed onto Brock's property?

Footsteps crunched on gravel, heading away, along with the cigarette smoke. Shadow motioned and she came forward to look. A man walked away from them down a gravel driveway toward a large house. To their left stood a big red barn, and to their right, another building that looked like a combination two-car garage with additional living quarters on top. Several cars were parked near the garage, but there was no sign of Heller's black Hummer.

"What if they're not here?" she whispered against his ear.

"Let's wait and watch for a bit." Shadow kept his eyes trained on the man, who went up onto the front porch of the house and lit another cigarette.

The man simply hung out on the porch smoking. Zoe guessed he was some kind of security guard, but there appeared to be no one else around. She looked again at the main house and wondered if Clare was inside. Movement at a second-floor window caught her eye.

"Clare!" she gasped.

***

CHAPTER ELEVEN

Tuesday Late Morning, Heller's Compound

Jason looked up to where Zoe pointed. The curtains in the upstairs window of Heller's house snapped closed.

"Clare was just there," Zoe whispered urgently in his ear. "But then she disappeared and the curtains closed."

Jason had been so focused on the guy on the front porch and scanning the grounds for more of Heller's men that he'd have missed Clarity if Zoe hadn't spotted her.

"Good, we've got confirmation she's here. Let go," he said.

They ran back through the trees and the hole in the fence. Jason grabbed the bolt cutters and leaned the cut section up over the hole, and then they hurried back to the truck.

Heller only has one guy watching the place. Weird, Jason thought as he fired up the engine. And where was Heller's Hummer? Was it in the garage or the barn, or was Heller not even there? That'd make rescuing Clarity a hell of a lot easier.

Zoe was uncharacteristically quiet. Jason glanced over at her as he drove toward Woodsville. She was looking out the window, her face pensive. No doubt, she was worried about her sister.

A short while later, they pulled up in front of Logjammers and parked beside several other pickups. Boon's VW bus wasn't there, but Jason wasn't surprised. The truck's clock indicated it was only just noon. He pushed through the swinging doors into Logjammers, Zoe on his heels.

Several men in baseball caps and plaid work shirts sat at a table eating lunch, while another couple guys sat at the bar drinking out of coffee mugs, one reading the local southern Humboldt County paper. Charlie stood behind the bar, cleaning the dust off a liquor bottle with a towel, his blue eyes zeroing in on them the instant they walked in the door.

Jason went to a table and pulled back a chair for Zoe.

"Why don't you have a seat and keep an eye out for Boon," he said. "I'll see if I can beg more food from Charlie while we wait."

"I'm not hungry." She sat down, her face tight.

"Don't worry. We'll get your sister," he said.

He turned and headed for Charlie, who put the bottle he'd been cleaning back on the shelf and then headed through the swinging doors into the kitchen. Jason joined him at the stainless steel kitchen counter.

"Hey, boyo," the grizzled old bartender said.

"Thanks for letting me borrow your truck. Any chance you could spot me another sub?"

Charlie nodded and pulled open a plastic bag of sandwich buns. He dropped his voice. "I got some info for you. Some guys were in here just a little while ago, five of 'em. Stuck out like sore thumbs, though they were trying hard to blend in. They were some kind of Feds, probably DEA, like a few years back." He scowled. "Anyway, they ordered some lunch and had their heads together, talking serious about something. I called Dan over at the gas station right after they left. He'd seen them, too. Told me they were driving those Fed cars, you know, big American sedans, both brand-spanking new."

"Interesting." The last time the DEA had come to town was still the stuff of legend and fueled the paranoia that persistently plagued the communities of southern Humboldt County.

Charlie gave him a knowing grin and nodded. No doubt the old guy had made his cover, but there was no point confirming it.

Jason made quickly for the rear of the tavern to the back alley. He had to share this new information with his boss. Porter answered on the first ring.

Jason jumped right in. "I have an eyewitness who saw the DEA in town this morning."

"Damn it, this is *our* fucking investigation!" Jason heard Porter slam a coffee mug down in the background. "You got anything new about the harvest timing?"

"Probably another week."

"We don't have another fucking week, not with the goddamned DEA moving in. Jesus—" Porter broke off and Jason could feel his frustration and anger pulsing through the line.

The task force had spent months setting up Heller's takedown, but their operation was small potatoes to the DEA, who didn't know or care about the bit players. Jason thought of Zoe and Clare and the other Seekers. If the Feds came in with their guns blazing and their usual heavy-handed tactics, no telling the collateral damage.

"I'm not going to let those bastards steal our show." Porter's voice broke through his thoughts. "Screw waiting for the harvest. We have to move up the timeline. Stay at the grow. Don't leave for a minute. The moment you spot Heller, call me, day or night. I'll have everyone in place for the bust by tomorrow."

"That soon? Heller may not be there."

"You know something?"

"He's with a young lady."

"What?"

"He's got one of the Seekers at his compound."

"How do you know?"

"I followed them."

"It's not your job to monitor his fucking social life, Parrish. You're there to bust him on drug trafficking, so get back to the grow. Got it?"

"Yes, sir." Jason hung up before Porter could say more. He was about to blatantly ignore his boss' orders. It was time to rescue Clarity.

#

Just minutes after Shadow followed the bartender into the kitchen, Zoe spotted Boon coming into the bar. She waved him over.

"Sorry it took so long." Boon sat down across from her at the table. "Where's Shadow?"

"Seeing if he can get us some food." Though how Shadow could think of food at a time like this, she couldn't imagine. Between being concerned for her sister and anxious about what they were about to attempt, she had no appetite.

Boon looked her solemnly in the eye. "I'm honored to help rescue your sister, Pele."

Zoe supposed she shouldn't be surprised about Boon's interest in her sister, but what was it about Clare and men? She attracted them like bees to a flower. A sweet, helpless flower.

"You know she's not well, right?" she said.

"Sol will help her." Boon spoke with the certainty of a true believer.

"No, he won't." Zoe's felt her frustration level rose. "I'm sorry, Boon, but New Age medicine and wishful thinking can only go so far. Her kidneys are deteriorating. If she goes into kidney failure, she could slip into a coma."

"A coma?" Boon looked surprised and concerned.

Maybe if she could convince him, he could work on convincing her sister.

"If you really care about her as much as you say you do, then you have to help me get her to a real, medical doctor," she said.

Boon looked at her for a long moment. To his credit, he seemed to seriously consider what she was saying, without Clare's or the other Seekers' denial.

"There are a lot of incompetent doctors," he said, finally. "And hospitals are dangerous places, filled with disease and germs, and death." His voice faded away and his expression saddened.

"It sounds like you're speaking from experience."

"My mom had cancer." Boon's shoulders slumped and he looked away.

Zoe wanted to know more, but the bartender came over.

"Here's your order." The old guy put a paper bag on the table and then headed over to the bar.

Where was Shadow? Zoe looked around and saw him coming from the hallway to the bathrooms.

"Glad to see you made it," he said to Boon and took a seat beside her.

"I came as fast as I could. Tell me, how can I help?"

Zoe felt herself warming to Boon. The guy seemed pretty level-headed and it was obvious he loved her sister.

Shadow looked at Boon. "I won't lie to you. What I'm going to ask you to do is dangerous. You got that?"

Boon nodded gravely.

Shadow laid out the plan, which involved Boon distracting Heller while they rescued Clare and then meeting up at Sunrise Camp.

"How should I get his attention?" Boon asked. "Do I just go up and ring his doorbell or something?"

"Try the keypad at the front gate. It's got a speaker on it. Make him come down. Do your best to stall him there, for as long as you can. Whatever you do, don't go near the house."

"That's where Clare is," Zoe said.

"And where we'll be." Shadow pushed back from the table. "It's going to be hard enough getting Clarity out safely. I don't want to have to worry about you, too."

"What should I say to Brock?" Boon looked worried.

"Stick to the truth: you're Clarity's boyfriend; you heard she was with him; you want to talk to her. Take your time explaining yourself," Shadow said.

"I can do that."

As Zoe thought about what Shadow said, she found herself having reservations. She turned to him. "What if things go wrong? Do you have a backup plan?"

"Worst case scenario, we call the cops. The important thing is to adapt as needed to the situation, be flexible." He paused for a moment, thinking. "If for some reason we all split up, let's meet at my sister's."

He gave Boon directions to both Brock's place and to JoAnn's.

Zoe and Shadow left Logjammers and drove to Brock's compound. A short while later, they reached the place on the dirt road where they'd parked before. Zoe watched Shadow shut off the truck. He reached across her to the glove compartment and popped it open.

"Don't freak out," he said, his face inches from hers, his eyes intense as he took out a lethal-looking black gun.

The way he expertly checked the magazine looked strangely familiar, but it was so out of character that it took her a moment to realize why.

Her dad used to do the exact same thing.

"Who are you?" She stared at him.

Everything about him suddenly shifted. The laid-back Seeker disappeared, despite his clothes and unkempt appearance. Zoe got feeling she was looking at a trained professional. He slid the weapon into his jacket.

"When this is all over, we'll talk." Shadow opened the driver-side door.

"You've got that right," she said as they got out of the truck.

"Want to change your mind and wait here?" He looked down at her and his expression softened for an instant.

"I'm coming," she said, but she wasn't an idiot. The stakes had just gone way up, now that she knew he had a gun.

#

Jason led Zoe back through the fence and onto Heller's property. When they reached the edge of the clearing inside the compound, Zoe came up beside him and nudged him hard in the ribs, pointing. Heller's

Hummer was now parked in front of the main house. Jason scowled. Rescuing Clarity had just gotten tougher. He glanced up at the upstairs curtains where Zoe had seen Clarity earlier, but they were still closed. The smoking guy had disappeared off the front porch. From their vantage point, Jason could see both the front and rear entrances to the house.

He turned to her and put his mouth against her ear, inhaling the soft scent of her hair as he whispered, "Let's head behind there." He pointed to the barn. It stood off to one side, less than fifteen feet from them. "We can sneak behind it to get closer to the house and the back door, but we've gotta move fast."

He led the way, dashing across the fifteen feet of open space. No bullets or shouts assaulted them as they reached the barn. The brush had been cut back, so nothing hampered their trip behind the barn. They had to pass a door half-way along the rear side of the barn, but fortunately it was closed. They made it to the corner of the barn closest to the house. The back door of the house lay no more than twenty feet ahead of them. So far, things were going smoothly.

Too smoothly, Jason's instincts warned.

Just then, the rumble of an engine broke the quiet. Gravel crunched under the wheels of a vehicle coming up the driveway. Jason snuck a look around the corner of the barn. Derrick Hanks' white pickup truck came into view on its way to the main house.

What was Hanks doing there?

The truck disappeared behind the front corner of the house. Jason gestured for Zoe to follow him. They were about to step out from the cover of the barn, when someone approached. He shoved her back.

"Heller, where you at? I gotta talk to you!" Hanks' voice bellowed.

"What you want with Heller?" said a male voice Jason didn't recognize.

"I got business with him. He's not picking up his damned phone."

"He don't want to be disturbed right now."

Jason stole another look around the corner of the barn. The smoker they'd seen on their initial stakeout stood in front of Hanks. He held a walkie-talkie in one hand. The other was in his pocket, which bulged ominously. It was obvious he had a gun.

"I'm not leaving 'til I talk to him," Hanks said, getting angry. "It's an emergency, goddamnit!"

"Better be." The guard switched on the walkie-talkie and radioed for Heller, his eyes on Hanks.

Moments later, Heller came from the front of the barn. Jason ducked his head back when Heller started to look around.

Was Clarity in the barn?

"I told you not to come here," Heller said.

"The fucking DEA's in town! You know, the Feds. I saw them when I was getting gas in Woodsville. Five guys. They ate at Logjammers. After that, I followed them to Garberville. Sure enough, they drove straight to the goddamn Sheriff's department. That's when I thought I'd better let you know."

"I already do. Get your guys and the rigs to the grow. The harvest's gotta go down now."

Jason wanted to stay and hear more, but they could use Hanks distracting Heller to check the barn for Clarity. He motioned Zoe to the barn's back door. He grasped the iron knob and slowly twisted. The simple wooden door opened, its hinges swinging easily on their well-oiled metal pegs, emitting no sound.

#

Why were they going into the barn, when Clare was in the house?

Shadow must have his reasons, Zoe thought, so she said nothing as the barn door swung open. She looked over his shoulder and peered around for some sign of her sister. Dust motes drifted about in the large space and the barn smelled of old grass and oil. Several pieces of farm equipment were stored there, including a tractor and some stacks of hay bales.

Most everything had the dust of ages on it, except a wall that sealed off one rear corner of the barn and created some kind of room. In the middle of the wall was a modern, standard-sized door. Both the wall and the door were brand new and bright white. They looked completely out of place in the rest of the unfinished wood barn.

"You think she's in there?" Zoe whispered.

"We have to check."

They moved quickly, hugging the rear wall and ducking behind the tractor and some other farm equipment on their way to the white door. Unease rippled through her when she saw its steel door knob gleaming dully in the dim light. There was something sinister about the small strange room built into the back of the barn. Why had Brock built it?

She held her breath as Shadow tried the knob, turning it, and pushing. The door didn't budge.

"What now?" she whispered.

"Keep an eye out." Shadow slipped a black case from inside his jacket.

"What're you doing?" she asked as he took out several small tools.

He ignored her and set to work on the lock. "Watch for Brock," he muttered.

He sure has a lot explaining to do, she thought as she crept toward the barn's front double doors. One of the double doors stood open. She sidled along the barn's wall, trying to keep out of sight of the open door. Outside, a truck engine fired up and started to roll away. Footsteps crunched closer. Someone was coming!

"Pssst!" she hissed to Shadow and pointed frantically toward the open barn door.

He glanced up from his work, calmly pocketed his tools, and then like a shadow melted away into the dim recesses at the back of the barn. He hid behind the old tractor. It was too far away for her to hide there.

Desperate, she looked around for a closer place to hide. Nowhere! There was nowhere close enough to hide. She pressed back against the wall, her heart hammering in her chest. If only she had her gun! There was nothing to do but pray Brock's eyes would need time to adjust to the low light level in the barn. He might miss her, if she kept absolutely still.

Brock came into the barn. He strode purposefully across to the locked door and didn't bother looking around. He removed a set of keys from his pants pocket and unlocked the door.

For an instant, she saw over his shoulder and into the room, bright with electric light, but then he closed the door behind him. The lock clicked into place. Silence. She strained her ears, listening, but no sound came from behind the locked door.

Was Clare in there? Wasn't Boon supposed to come and distract Brock?

Somewhere outside in the distance overhead, a hawk screamed, but beyond that, the late afternoon was quiet. She hurried over to Shadow, who was moving stealthily toward the white door. He had his gun out. She leaned against him and put her mouth to his ear.

"What're you doing?"

"We have to get Brock out of there."

"What about Boon?"

Shadow shook his head sharply. His shoulders were rigid with tension. "Forget Boon. We have to get Heller out. Now."

She clutched his shoulder, dread welling up. "Why?"

He started to push her arm off when the door clicked, unlocking. They jumped back and dove behind the tractor just as the door opened and Brock appeared.

***

CHAPTER TWELVE

Tuesday Afternoon, Heller's Compound

Jason crouched beside Zoe behind the tractor. Glancing around the front wheel, he watched Heller pause in the open doorway of that strange room inside the barn. The walkie-talkie attached to Heller's belt beeped. Heller unclipped it and raised it to his mouth.

"Be right there," he said. He looked over his shoulder. "Don't go anywhere."

Beyond him inside the room, a woman moaned.

Clarity!

Jason raised his gun and sighted down the barrel. His finger on the trigger tingled with the urge to shoot the bastard. Zoe grabbed his forearm. Her fingers squeezed, hard. He glared at her, but she glared right back.

Damn, she was keeping her cool, but he wasn't.

The realization sobered him. He nodded and acknowledged her silent command. He slowly lowered his gun and she released her hold on him. Heller locked the door and left the barn, just as a vehicle approached on the gravel drive.

Maybe that was Boon coming, maybe not, but it was time to get Clarity out of there.

Jason leapt to his feet and raced across to the modern, white door. He tucked the gun in his pocket and pulled out his lock picks. The lock was a new Schlage, trivial to open. It took him under thirty seconds.

"How did you learn to do that?" Zoe whispered.

"Long story." He opened the door.

"Clare!" Zoe stifled a cry and rushed past him to her sister.

Rage filled him when he saw Clarity in the bright electric light. She sat on a metal chair with the sleeve on her right arm rolled above her elbow. Her long blond hair streamed down her back and her head lolled sideways, as though she were falling asleep. Her eyes were unfocused under heavy eyelids.

Beside her on a stainless steel table lay a syringe, along with some black rubber tubing, a plastic bag containing a light-colored powder, and a small metal bowl. He went over and touched his fingertip to the surface of the bowl and then to the tip of his tongue. The slightly bitter, vitamin taste was instantly, unpleasantly familiar. It looked like Heller had already injected Clarity with heroin, but with how much? Would her body be able to process it, given her kidney problems?

He scanned the room. Heller had lost his fascination with medieval ironwork and replaced his collection of S&M toys with a whole new assortment of leather and steel and devices.

He wished he could arrest the bastard on the spot, but now wasn't the time. There was at least one armed guy outside the barn, and Heller was undoubtedly packing heat, to. He couldn't risk the safety of the two sisters.

"What's wrong with her?" Zoe whispered to him, fear loud in her voice.

"She's doped up on heroin."

All the telltale signs were there. Clarity's pupils had shrunk to the size of pinpoints.

"What did that bastard do to you!" Zoe hissed at her.

"Brock? He just gave me some medicine to make me feel better."

Zoe tried to get her to stand up. "We've got to get you out of here."

"I'm OK, just feeling a little dizzy." Clarity stumbled.

"I've got her," Jason said.

Zoe stepped out of the way. He swung Clarity into his arms. She felt too light, as if she were merely skin and bones. Her head lolled back against his shoulder and she seemed to go unconscious. Zoe rushed ahead of them to the door but then stopped.

She turned, her eyes wide. "Brock!"

"Come on!" Jason rushed past her with Clarity.

They cleared the threshold of the room and into the much dimmer barn. Zoe closed the door behind them as they raced through the shadows toward the rear door, but they'd run out of time.

"Dude, I don't want to put you out or anything," said Boon.

Jason got Clarity behind the tractor just as Heller appeared with Boon, coming in the barn's open double door. Zoe ducked down beside them in the nick of time.

"I mean, really, dude." Boon hadn't stopped talking. His words cascaded over themselves in a torrent. "Thanks for offering. Of course I'd love a hit of your shit, Brock, like I said, thanks for offering. I'm sure it's fantastic, absolutely fantastic. But I understand if you're busy, you being such an important dude and all. You really don't need to go to all the trouble, 'cause I know how much stuff you've got going on, and stuff. I mean, really, dude."

Jason had to give Boon credit for trying to stall Heller, but what the hell was Heller doing, bringing him to the barn?

Heller slid the barn's double doors closed and advanced on Boon. "You've wasted enough of my time. Why are you really here?"

"Dude, I'm not trying to waste your time, honest to God, I'm not. I was hoping I could just maybe see my girlfriend for a minute, you know, Clarity, because I really miss her. Maybe we could go back outside now?" Boon tried to move around Heller toward the doors.

Heller reached under his coat and pulled out a gun. He pointed it at Boon. "Stop. Now."

Boon spun around. Seeing the gun, he shot his hands up in the air. "Dude! No need for violence, really. Come on, man, I'll just be on my way." His words picked up tempo, fear driving them.

Damn it, things were getting out of hand.

Jason needed his hands free, but Clarity was a dead weight hampering him. He lay her down beside Zoe behind the tractor. Unfortunately, Boon stood just beyond Heller in his line of fire, so using his gun was out.

"Clarity is *not* your girlfriend," Heller said flatly.

"But I love her. Can't I just see her for a moment, maybe talk to her or something?" Boon's voice quavered.

"You're pathetic, Seeker. At least you can die like a real man—" Heller raised the gun.

Jason jumped to his feet. He stepped out from behind the tractor. "Stop, Heller."

Heller pivoted, training his gun on Jason. His eyes narrowed in recognition. "Parrish. What the fuck are you doing here?"

#

Zoe clutched Clare against her side as she peeked around the tractor. It took everything she had to keep from charging out to distract Brock, or Heller, as Shadow was calling him. Anything, to keep that lethal-looking gun off Shadow.

"It's time someone stopped you, Heller," Shadow said, his voice harsh and threatening. He sounded nothing like the Seeker she'd gotten to know.

"You, stop me? Don't make me laugh." Heller kept his eyes on Shadow, who slowly circled to the side, away from where she and Clare were hiding and away from Boon, who stood frozen in place, his eyes hunting for them in the shadows of the dim barn.

Zoe tore her eyes from the confrontation and looked at her sister sitting on the barn floor beside her. Was she lucid enough to escape? They had to try while the two men faced off.

Zoe draped her sister's arm over her shoulders and hoisted her to standing.

"Let's go," she whispered.

Clare nodded and her feeble grip on Zoe's shoulders tightened. Zoe wrapped one of her own arms securely around Clare's waist and hoisted her to standing. They made awkward progress, heading away from the men toward the barn's rear door. The shadowy lighting inside the barn was deepening with the afternoon. The men were so focused on each other, Zoe hoped their escape would go unnoticed.

"You killed my sister, you sick, twisted bastard," Shadow was saying to Heller.

"That what you think?" Heller sniggered. "She didn't get what she didn't want, Parrish. Wasn't my fault she OD'd."

"I'm going to make sure you never kill anyone ever again."

"You're in no position to make threats, Parrish, and you're wasting my time. I think I'll just shoot the two of you useless potheads and be done with it."

"No!" Boon shouted.

Zoe glanced over her shoulder and saw Boon launch himself at Heller, his arm wildly karate-chopping at the gun in a desperate act of bravado. The motion propelled Heller's arm downward and the muzzle dropped away from Shadow to the barn floor. Shadow seized the moment and jumped Heller, knocking the gun out of his hands. Heller raised his fists and took a swing at Shadow, who blocked and counterpunched. They began trading vicious blows.

Why didn't Shadow pull his gun? Had he lost it when he jumped Heller?

Boon spotted Zoe and Clare and rushed toward them. Suddenly, a gunshot blasted. Zoe shoved Clare down behind the hay bales near the barn's rear door. The bullet missed Boon by inches and rammed into the wall of the barn directly above them. Wood splinters flew from the bullet's impact as Boon dropped to his stomach on the floor just feet from where Zoe and Clare crouched.

Zoe risked a peek around the hay bales and saw with horror that Shadow sat on the ground behind Heller, looking dazed. Heller held the gun again, but he was looking at Boon, who was wriggling on his belly across the floor toward Zoe and her sister. As she watched,

Heller raised his gun. He was going to shoot Boon in the back!

Zoe reached out an arm and grabbed Boon's hand to help him. Sound exploded again, and simultaneously pain ripped through her right arm as Boon reached the safety of the hay bales. She clamped her mouth shut against a cry. No way she was going to let Heller know he'd hit her.

Her arm burned with pain. Gingerly, she moved it, assessing the injury. It throbbed, and she felt the wetness of blood, but it seemed like maybe she was only grazed. It didn't feel like the bullet was still inside.

"You OK?" Boon whispered, his eyes wide as he looked at her injured arm.

She nodded and glanced at Clare. "Take her to JoAnn's. She needs a doctor. We'll meet you there."

Zoe heard Shadow challenge Heller. "That's how cowards fight, shooting an unarmed man when he's down."

Was Heller going to shoot Shadow?

She risked another glance around the hay bales. With relief, she saw that Shadow was on his feet, struggling with Heller for the gun.

"Go out that way," she whispered to Boon and pointed at the rear barn door, not more than five feet away. "Watch out for Heller's guard. He's out there somewhere."

"What about you?"

"Just get her to safety!" No way was she going to leave Shadow to fight Heller alone.

Boon lifted Clare into his arms and made a mad rush for the door. They escaped outside. Zoe turned her focus to Shadow. He moved like his Seeker name, a shadowy silhouette in the dim light, as he fought Heller. He was taller than Heller, but Heller was a ruthless bundle of muscles, spinning a sudden kick that knocked Shadow to his knees. Heller jumped him and got him in a chokehold as Shadow struggled to get back to his feet. Shadow plucked at Heller's arm, trying unsuccessfully to dislodge it. He abruptly keeled forward. The violent motion flipped Heller over his shoulders. The two men squared off, fists raised.

Where were the guns? Both Heller's and Shadow's guns had disappeared. Zoe scanned the barn floor, but she couldn't see them in the dim light.

Suddenly Heller scooped a handful of dirt from the floor and threw it into Shadow's face, using the tactic to launch an offensive of savage blows to Shadow's ribs.

She had to do something!

She frantically looked around for some kind of weapon. She spotted a big metal hook leaning against the wall behind her. It was long, sharp, and made of steel. She grabbed it and charged Heller, not sure what she was going to do, but anything to stop him from hurting Shadow.

"Leave him alone!" she shouted as Heller knocked Shadow to the ground and prepared to kick him in the head.

Heller looked up, his foot planting harmlessly back down on the ground. "Ah, the redhead. You as hot as your hair, Red?"

He took a threatening step toward her. Zoe gripped the hook with both hands, ignoring the stabbing pain in her right upper arm. She held the hook defensively at waist level.

"Shut up, you creep!"

Heller grinned, his perfect white teeth bright in the dim light. He snaked out an arm to grab the hook, but

Zoe thrashed it savagely through the air and caught the side of his hand, slicing him.

"You fucking bitch!" He howled with rage and frustration, unable to attack while she continued to lash out at him with the hook.

She sensed Shadow circling them, but she didn't dare take her eyes off Heller, who suddenly jerked his hands over his head. Was that fear in those flat, black eyes?

"Shadow?" she called out, her gaze still on Heller.

"You can put that down now, Pele," Shadow said as he came to stand beside her, his gun leveled at Heller.

"Pele here believes in the law and the rules that make society civilized," Shadow nodded his head at her, "but you and I know how the system really works, don't we? Those who have the money and the power can use and abuse those who are weaker."

"Hell yeah, man. It's survival of the fittest. Eat or be eaten." Heller thrust out his chest, his overdeveloped muscles bunching under the thin nylon of his T-shirt. He started to lower his hands. Zoe could see the blood from where she'd cut him trickling down toward his elbow.

"Keep your hands up, Heller." Shadow motioned upward with his gun. "You're not going to hurt anyone, ever again. It's time someone stopped you, permanently."

"Pretty speech, Parrish, but you don't have the guts." He spat in the dirt at Shadow's feet.

Zoe glanced at Shadow and realized with gut-wrenching certainty that he was ready to shoot Heller. "Don't listen to him, Shadow! You're no murderer, and it won't bring your sister back."

She reached out and placed a hand gently on his gun arm. "Don't throw your life away for this scumbag. He doesn't deserve it. He'll pay, just not right now. Let's get the hell out of here!"

#

Jason fought the conflicting urges raging inside him, the need for vengeance against the need to uphold the law. He kept his gun on Heller, who stood poised on the balls of his feet, ready to attack if he let down his guard for a second.

Zoe was right. Killing Heller wouldn't bring Tammy back, but it'd be so satisfying to pull the trigger and finish Heller off, once and for all.

But would that end it, really? There'd be the corpse to deal with, the evidence. He could claim it was self-defense, but then he'd have made Zoe a witness or possibly even an accessory to the crime.

Another option raced through him. He could arrest Heller for kidnapping, but as soon as he considered it, he dismissed it. There were too many variables. He had no backup, and he'd blow his cover with Heller. He wanted to make damned sure that when he busted Heller, he'd make it stick.

"Come on, Shadow!" Zoe's voice broke through his thoughts. She was moving to the barn's open rear door.

Jason backed away, his gun steady on Heller.

"I'm not done with you," he said, tamping down his frustration at having to let the bastard go. "You *will* pay."

The moment he cleared the barn's threshold, Jason turned and ran.

Heller's shouts echoed after him. "You'd better run like the fucking wind, Parrish, 'cause I'm gonna get you!"

Jason sprinted after Zoe, away from the barn across the cleared grassy area, and into the safety of the trees. A powerful engine roared to life behind them at the main house. They dashed the short distance through the trees to the dirt service road that ran along the fence bordering Heller's property. Jason started to cross the road when Zoe grabbed him by the back of his jacket.

"What's that?" she whispered, pointing down the road.

The rumbling growl of the approaching vehicle had to be Heller's Hummer.

"Come on," he said and raced across the road to the fence, Zoe on his heels.

They scrambled through the hole. He paused long enough to stick the cut section of fence back over the hole. If someone was looking, the cut in the fence was obvious, but maybe they'd get lucky.

They hurried through the last stretch of forest toward Pete's truck. Jason spotted the bright sheen of the white pickup through the trees, not more than twenty feet away, but beyond it, he sensed the hulking blackness of the Hummer.

"What is it?" Zoe came up beside him.

He held up his hand for silence. The late afternoon light created long shadows and further hampered visibility through the dense stand of second and third growth trees, but he knew Heller was somewhere over there. He strained to hear anything suspicious.

Leaves crackled behind them. He looked back over his shoulder, beyond Zoe, who stood directly behind him, her eyes wide with alarm. Whoever was on their tail was still out of sight, but the leaves crunched again, louder.

"Come on!" Zoe whispered, starting forward.

Jason shot out his hand to stop her, mentally running through their options. They couldn't go forward, and they couldn't go back. They could make a beeline for the main road, but they'd be easy targets out in the open. The only option was to head east, into the hills.

He signaled for her to follow and they started off, pushing through the underbrush growing under the trees. There was no way to avoid the rustling, swishing branches of the bushes and their footsteps crunching on leaves.

"They're over there!" the man following them shouted.

Bushes crashed nearby as Heller closed in on them from the side. Jason tensed, expecting bullets to whiz by. They had to get the hell out of there. Fast. He launched forward at a dead run, shoving branches and tangled overgrowth out of the way and hoped Zoe could keep up.

A good distance farther, the trees grew larger and the undergrowth more sparse. He looked back and slowed his pace. Zoe was falling behind. He stopped and waited. When she caught up, he listened for their pursuers. The early evening was warm, peaceful, and quiet. He exhaled with relief. They were alone in the deep forest, at least for now.

"We have to keep going," he said softly.

She leaned against the trunk of a tall pine, cradling her right arm. In the dim light, he saw where Heller's bullet had torn a gash in the upper right arm of her jacket.

"You OK?" he asked.

"I've been shot."

***

CHAPTER THIRTEEN

Tuesday Evening, Humboldt Forest

Zoe pushed away from the tree where she'd momentarily stopped to rest. The sun had set and twilight was falling over the forest. Her upper right arm throbbed with pain. Shadow looked down at her with concern.

"I think the bullet only grazed me," she said.

Shadow cursed under his breath as he bent to take a closer look at where the bullet had torn through her jacket sleeve and ripped into her upper arm.

"Based on how little you're bleeding, I think you're right about the bullet just grazing you, but I won't know for sure until I can take a better look. Can you move it?" he asked, his eyes intent as he watched her.

She gingerly lifted her arm. "Yes, but it hurts." The intense pain she'd felt when first shot had diminished to a dull nagging.

"I'll bet it does," he said gently.

His voice was so full of caring and sympathy that she fought back tears. Now wasn't the time to fall apart, not when they were on the run in the wilds of the Humboldt forest, but the adrenaline was wearing off from their escape and she was beginning to feel a little overwhelmed.

She remembered those crazed moments when Boon dashed from the barn with Clare in his arms. "You think Clare and Boon made it safely to JoAnn's? I told him to take her there."

"I don't see why not," Shadow said. "From what Heller said, all his men except that one guard are at the Garden, and we didn't hear any other gunshots or anything. We also know that Heller and most likely that guard were busy chasing us into the woods and not chasing your sister and Boon."

Zoe let out a long breath she didn't even realize she'd been holding. He was probably right.

"Which way to Sunrise Camp?" She looked up at the somber wall of trees surrounding them. There was no sign of a trail and she had no idea where they were. She looked at Shadow and realized exactly how much she depended on him. It wasn't a familiar sensation and she wasn't sure she liked it.

Shadow was still looking down at her arm. "First thing is to take care of your injury."

"How? We're in the middle of nowhere," she said, despair welling up.

She bit back a sob, furious at feeling so helpless, but it was too late. Hot tears slid down her cheeks. She swiped them angrily away with her good hand.

"Come here," he murmured and carefully enclosed her uninjured body in a hug. "You're so brave. I can't believe you didn't tell me you were shot sooner."

"There wasn't time. Besides, I told you, it's just a flesh wound."

171

"And you know what a flesh wound feels like, right?" he laughed, his body rumbling against hers.

"No, now I do." She rubbed her face against his jacket, inhaling the scent of mountains and forest and man. It was a good smell, reassuring.

He held her, and for a moment, she felt the trees, dark and quiet around them.

"We're not being followed anymore, are we?" she said finally.

"No, we're safe." Shadow dropped his arms from her and took a step back.

He looked up at the stars that were starting to pop out in the evening sky.

"I know a place we can go. It's an old hunting cabin that used to belong to my grandfather. My cousin Arnie owns it now. I haven't been there in years, so I'm not sure what condition it's in, but my grandpa always used to keep first aid supplies there. It's somewhere up this canyon, not too far. You OK to walk now?"

"Yes," she said. Anything was better than standing still in the quickly darkening forest.

He moved away from her and into the trees. She followed, and after a short distance, they came to an old dirt road. It felt good to be out of the dense forest and where there was more light from the sky. Shadow stopped and looked both ways and then up at the sky again, as if he could read a map there.

He turned to the right and Zoe followed him along the road. It hadn't been used in a long time. Branches and rocks had fallen across it, and in places they had to climb over downed trees. They headed steadily uphill, following a drainage that sloped away to their left. They came to a junction with another old dirt road, and this time Shadow didn't pause but continued forward with purpose, as if he recognized where they were.

Zoe tamped down her fatigue, but the road seemed endless, the mountain enormous, and the moonless night seemed to grow darker by the moment. They scrambled over more fallen trees and around boulders that had rolled across the old road. Her injured arm complained with the effort. They passed a few more junctions but always kept heading up the canyon.

Finally, the trees thinned into a small clearing. The stars shone bright overhead. They had climbed far enough upward that the canyon had shrunk to a small swale. A creek gurgled somewhere nearby.

"We're here," Shadow said and strode toward an old wood cabin that loomed in the dark. "I'll be right back." He disappeared around the side of it.

Someone had built a rough-hewn log bench in front of the cabin. She wearily took a seat and waited, feeling her injured arm throb. Several minutes later, he returned.

"We're in luck," he said. "My grandpa never wanted to come up here and forget the key, so he always kept one hidden. I guess Arnie's kept up the tradition."

He fiddled with a small metal can that rattled in his hands and then pulled out a key. He unlocked the padlock securing the cabin and swung open the door. It creaked on old hinges, releasing the musty smell of dust and age.

"There should be a flashlight somewhere around here," he said, stepping inside and fumbling just inside the door.

A moment later, he switched on a flashlight. She followed him into the cabin, the flashlight beam bouncing around the place. He struck a match and an oil lantern spluttered to life. It filled the cabin with a soft, warm light. A rustic river rock fireplace stood at one end of the room with an old couch in front of it. There was a tiny kitchen area with a table and chairs. Bookshelves along one wall housed board games and a few tattered books.

She crossed the room to look through the door at the far end. Inside was a sleeping area. Two sets of bunk beds stood across from each other with a big bed in between.

"There's a sleeping loft, too," Shadow said. He pointed to a ladder that led though an opening in the ceiling. "We used to all pile in here during hunting season, back in the day. My grandpa and my dad would bring my brother Richard and me up, and sometimes Uncle Joe and Cousin Arnie and his two younger brothers."

She sat down on one of the wood chairs beside the table as Shadow went to the kitchen area.

"Good news," he said. "It looks like Arnie hasn't changed much. There should be a first aid kit around here."

While Shadow rooted around in the cabinet under the counter, she took stock of her injury in the lantern light. The sight of bloody ripped leather made her quickly turn her head away.

"Did you and your family hunt deer?" she asked, trying to take her mind off her arm.

"Supposedly." His voice lost its nostalgic tone. "Actually, we kids mostly ended up on our own, while my dad and the other men sat around and drank themselves into oblivion. No one ever brought back a deer, not that I remember. Here we go."

He pulled a box of first aid supplies from the cabinet under the counter and set them on the table beside Zoe.

"OK, let's see your arm." He looked at the bloody gash and how it had ripped through her jacket and his face darkened. "We're going to need a few more things before getting you patched up."

He went and picked up a big plastic bucket that sat on the floor by the front door. "My grandpa always planned to install running water, but he never got around to it. I'm going to get some water from the creek in case we need it."

While he was gone, Zoe listened to the silence. She tried to imagine Shadow as a child in the cabin with the men of his family, but her brain was fuzzy with fatigue. The quiet was so loud that her ears rang. The oil lamp spluttered briefly, its light wavering for a moment. It gave off a faint chemical smell.

Shadow came back and put the bucket of water on the floor beside the table. "I wonder if there's still some hooch around here."

He went to the bookshelf by the fireplace where an old green glass gallon wine jug sat on the bottom shelf. A little liquid sloshed around in it when he put it on the table.

"We're in luck." He uncorked the jug and poured a measure into one of the brown ceramic coffee mugs. He handed it to her. "Like whiskey?"

"Not really." She sniffed the stuff. It smelled foul and made her eyes water.

He watched her. "It's hooch, definitely nothing fancy, but it'll take the edge off."

"Here goes nothing." She swigged back the whiskey in one giant swallow. It felt like knives cutting her throat. She started coughing. The spasms wrenched her wound painfully.

"You don't mess around," Shadow chuckled, taking the mug.

He scooped water from the bucket on the floor and handed the mug to her. She drank the soothing water with relief.

#

Jason watched Zoe finish the water. Again and again, she surprised him with her ability to face down whatever crisis was thrown at them, like getting shot. The next task wasn't going to be pleasant, but after everything they'd gone through together, he knew she could handle it.

He poured more whiskey into the mug and held it out to her. "Another?"

"I'm OK. Let's get this over with." She started to struggle out of her jacket, wincing with the effort.

He put the mug on the table, stood up, and stepped behind her. She turned on her chair so he could take hold of her jacket around the collar and carefully slide it down her good arm. The leather was soft and supple under his fingers.

"OK so far?" he asked.

She nodded.

"Here goes the other one." He inched her jacket down off her injured arm.

Blood still oozed from the gash across the outer edge of her bicep. It had fused the jacket to her blouse and the flesh of upper her arm. Her breath caught as he pulled the jacket free.

"Sorry," he muttered, feeling relieved when the jacket slid easily the rest of the way off. Her hands moved to the buttons of her blouse.

"Need help?" he asked, but then saw how her breasts curved under the thin material. He cleared his throat, his mouth suddenly dry.

"I think I've got it," she said. Her fingers flicked the final button and her blouse gaped open.

Hastily, he turned away, her jacket gripped in his hands. He stared blankly at the first aid supplies on the table, all his senses attuned to what she was doing.

She's been through enough, so keep your mind out of the gutter, he told himself, but he heard the soft whisper of her blouse slide off her skin and a flash of her bare arm caught his eye as she laid her blouse on the chair. His heart beat too heavily in his chest.

"I don't think I need stitches. Do you?" she asked.

Her question broke through his paralysis. He put her jacket down and grabbed the bottle of isopropyl alcohol. He poured a little over his hands and then turned around to treat her injury. What he got was a full view of her breasts, screened behind a beige bra that gave the illusion she wasn't wearing one. He swallowed, his throat suddenly dry.

"What do you think?" She looked up and caught his expression. "You OK? You aren't afraid of blood or something, are you?"

He shook his head, clearing his throat, and forced his eyes to closely examine the wound. He let out a long, slow breath. "You're one lucky lady. Another inch over and the bullet could have severed the main artery in your arm. Several inches more, and well—"

A couple of inches over and the bullet would have gone straight through her heart. He handed her the mug of whiskey. "You'd better have a little more, because cleaning it is going to really hurt."

She took the mug, grimaced, and drank the whiskey in another big gulp. He picked up the bottle of isopropyl alcohol.

"Take my hand," he said, holding her good hand with his. "Now squeeze. Squeeze as hard as you can."

He began to pour the antiseptic slowly over her wound, washing the gash clean.

"God damn!" Her whole tensed against the pain.

She gripped him with her good hand, her nails biting into him. Her eyes were huge, her pupils dilated, but she gave him a small, careful smile when he finished.

"Thanks. Squeezing helped."

"That's because you feel less pain if you're distracted by doing something else. Let's get you bandaged up."

He closed the bottle of antiseptic and gathered the supplies while she dried the area around the wound with the cotton swab. He taped a bandage securely around her bicep.

"Almost as good as new, right?" he asked.

She looked at her bloody blouse lying on the chair. "I'd love a clean shirt."

"Easy. Good thing I dress in layers." He unbuttoned the plaid flannel shirt he wore over his rainbow tie-dye T-shirt and handed it to her.

"You don't mind?" she asked, sliding her good arm into its sleeve.

"I'd take off my shirt for you anytime you ask," he grinned.

He hadn't meant it to sound suggestive, but she laughed. "A true knight in shining armor, huh?"

If you only knew, he thought, trying not to watch as she buttoned up his shirt.

It was way too big and hung down to her thighs. She looked tousled and wonderful and his fingers tingled with the urge to undo her buttons.

"You think there's anything to eat around here?" she said, starting to stand up.

"Relax." He put a hand on her shoulder, staying her movement. "You're my patient. Let me take care of you."

"I'm not helpless." She took his hand and squeezed it gently before letting go. "Why don't you make a fire. I'll see about finding us some dinner."

Definitely not helpless, he thought as he watched her move to the cabinet over the sink.

He tore his eyes from her and went to the fireplace. When he'd first remembered the cabin, he'd been focused solely on getting her first aid, but now that they were safe, he couldn't stop thinking about the two of them alone together. They had the whole night ahead of them. He built a good-sized fire while Zoe heated a can of chili on the propane stove.

"Hungry?" she asked as she dished out the food.

Not that kind of hungry, he thought, going to the table.

He took a seat and then looked up. She was gazing down at him. His heartbeat kicked up as the moment stretched and she didn't look away. He found himself staring at her mouth. She moved closer and dipped her head. She brushed her mouth over his in a whisper of a kiss.

"I've wanted to do that since I fed you that sub in the truck."

She smiled and it lit up her face like the sun, the radiant force of it compelling him closer. He leaned in and traced her jawline from her chin to her ear, spreading his fingers into her luxuriant hair. He pulled back for another chaste kiss, but she had other plans. The teasing touch of her tongue called for him to come out and play. His heart slammed up against his ribs as the kiss deepened, but soon it wasn't enough. He needed to feel her body against his.

He ended the kiss and stood up. Taking her good hand in his, he led her to the couch by the fire. The room was warm from the blaze. He pulled the T-shirt off over his head. She watched him standing before her, her eyes on his chest, and he felt his skin stroked by her gaze. Her hands went to the buttons of the flannel shirt.

"Let me." He knelt on the floor in front of her and unbuttoned the shirt.

"Thanks for taking care of my arm and for helping rescue my sister and for everything," she said as he unclasped her bra.

Her breasts were perfect.

"Anytime," he exhaled long and low.

"Shadow," she sighed as he took them in his hands.

"Jason, my name is Jason," he muttered as she pulled him to her for another kiss.

She was fire and molten heat, simmering in his arms, kissing him with an intensity that threatened a firestorm. Without breaking the kiss, he joined her on the couch and pulled her on top of him. She was a welcome weight, her body supple and pliant. Her legs straddled him, scorching him where his body burned.

He wrenched his mouth free of hers. "You sure about this?"

"You have to ask?" She moved against him, her eyes dark with sensual awareness.

"A gentleman always asks, but when you put it that way, your wish is my command," he grinned.

Careful of her injured arm, he cast himself into her fire, willing and ready to let himself burn.

#

Zoe stroked the crisp hair on Shadow's chest.

Jason, not Shadow, she reminded herself, but she wasn't yet ready to think about the implications of what had just happened between them.

She wanted to stay in the moment, just the two of them, alone together, and revel in how good it felt to be warm and safe, and thoroughly, languorously sated. Her stomach grumbled.

"Hungry?" Jason asked.

She looked down the length of his body and her body hummed with renewed desire. She laughed with pleasure. "Looks like you're hungry, too."

"Dinner can wait a little longer, right?" His eyes glinted in the firelight.

Some time later, she roused herself enough to look up from their entangled bodies and across at the stove.

"No question our dinner's cold now." She gave him a quick kiss before getting off the couch and standing up.

"The delay was totally worth it." He tucked his hands behind his head and she felt him watching her.

The air in the room felt cool on her bare skin. She carefully pulled the flannel shirt on, over her injured arm. His scent engulfed her as she buttoned it, patchouli and wood smoke and Jason. She inhaled the exotic scents as she finished dressing, her fingers still tingling from the feel of him. His muscular body had been a welcome surprise under his baggy Seeker clothes. She finished dressing and went to reheat their dinner while Jason tended the fire.

After a quick, companionably silent meal, they sat together on the couch. The fire crackled cheerfully in the fireplace and the room grew so deliciously warm that she had trouble keeping her eyes open. She leaned against him and closed her eyes. He hadn't put on his T-shirt and she listened to the comforting beat of his heart where her ear rested against his warm skin.

"We've been so busy coping and dealing and trying to help your sister, you never really told me much about yourself." His deep voice rumbled against her ear. "What was it like growing up in the desert?"

"Not much to tell, really," she yawned and nestled closer to him, feeling utterly relaxed and completely exhausted.

She didn't want to talk about the past, or anything. She just wanted to slip into sleep and deal with it all in the morning.

"Happy childhood," she said, yawning again. "Then later my folks were killed in a car accident, and then I moved to San Francisco."

"What about your sister?"

Why does it always have to come back to Clare?

She sighed, but not with pleasure. "She's had kidney problems since we were kids."

"Lots of people have kidney problems, but they don't turn out like Clarity. Why did she get involved with the Seekers?"

Why does he have to keep pushing?

She pulled away from him and sat up. She turned and looked at him, wondering again about all his contradictions.

"What about you, 'Shadow?'" She made quotation marks with her fingers. "Or is it 'Jason'?" she said, recalling his passionate demand. "Why are you out here in the woods, hanging out in a pot cult? What are you running from?"

"I'm not running from anything." He pushed himself off the couch and went to the fire, his back to her as he poked at the logs with a rusty piece of rebar.

She turned her gaze away from the strong planes of his back and the long, lean lines of his body. How could she have hooked up with him, a Seeker who hung out homeless in the woods? Their lives were literally worlds apart. Tomorrow, she'd go get Clare from his sister's and they'd leave for San Francisco. She'd probably never see him again.

Exhaustion and everything that had happened since coming to Humboldt crashed down on her. She squeezed her eyes shut against the hot prick of tears. When she opened them again, he was fully clothed and banking the fire.

"Let's get some sleep," he said. "Tomorrow's going to be another long day."

***

CHAPTER FOURTEEN

Wednesday Morning, Humboldt Forest

Jason stood at the old propane stove in his grandpa's cabin, stirring the oatmeal as he waited for Zoe to wake up. Yesterday had not gone as planned. He was supposed to be tracking Heller and preparing for the drug bust. Instead, he'd had to rescue Clarity and Heller had shot Zoe. He glanced over at the couch, remembering last night. Yesterday hadn't been all bad. Not at all, but Zoe still didn't know who he really was.

As if his thoughts conjured her, Zoe came into the room, her curly hair tousled about her head, his flannel shirt hanging to her thighs. Desire hit him so hard in the gut that he had to look away. He turned back to the stove.

"Good morning. Coffee?" He poured a steaming mug and handed it to her. "How's your arm?"

"Almost as good as new. Thanks for helping me with it last night," she smiled.

"I liked helping you. You need some help this morning?" Try as he might, he couldn't stop thinking about them together.

She laughed and took a sip of her coffee. "I don't need help, but boy this coffee does. It's lousy."

"It's one of those canned coffee brands. It was already open and probably a few years old, but better than nothing, right?"

"I'm not so sure." She grimaced but took another sip.

He dished out two bowls of oatmeal. "This stuff's old, too, but I doubt oatmeal ages as badly as coffee."

He found a couple of paper packets of sugar in the cardboard shoebox of spices his grandpa kept on the shelf above the kitchen counter. He handed one to Zoe and sprinkled the other on his oatmeal. They took the bowls over to the table and sat down.

Jason wasn't sure how to tackle what had to be said. He chewed the gummy oatmeal, thinking. She didn't seem to want to talk, either, but they had to.

He jumped in. "We need to talk about last night."

"No, we don't." She kept eating and wouldn't look at him.

"Yes, we do. We can't let our personal issues get in the way, not if we're going to help your sister, or if we have to stand against Heller again."

"We had sex, so what? It meant nothing." She got up from the table and went to put her bowl in the sink.

She didn't mean that!

He jumped up and followed her. He wasn't going to let her push him away. Last night had been something special. They'd connected.

He stroked a finger lightly down her cheek and then gently eased her into his arms. "You really want to tell me you're the 'love 'em and leave 'em' type?"

"I'm not, but it doesn't matter. I'll be leaving today with Clare and that's that, right?" She leaned back in his arms and looked up at him.

Frustration but also desire simmered in her eyes. Her mouth beckoned him. He couldn't resist the impulse. He dipped his head and pressed his lips to hers. She returned the kiss and instantly the fire flared again between them, rising up, engulfing them. For a moment, he forgot everything but the feel, the taste, the scent of her, but then just as quickly, reality came crashing back. He pulled back.

What the hell am I doing? She has no idea who I really am.

She was looking up at him with all kinds of emotion on her face, her beautiful eyes wide, her cheeks flushed.

He cursed, unable to stop his body from remembering every instant of when she'd lain against him, over him, under him. The hunger gnawed at him, and even now, he felt himself respond.

Pushing away from her, he ran his hands through his shaggy hair and started to pace the cabin's short span of floor, reminding himself that his whole mission was about to come to a head with the harvest. He couldn't afford to be distracted, but he couldn't let her leave thinking he was a drugged out Seeker, either.

What if I tell her the truth? The tempting thought whispered through him as he paced.

His job demanded a cover story. He had to appear convincing to the Seekers and to Heller, but—he pivoted and paced the other direction—she was going to leave today, anyway, so maybe he wouldn't risk too much telling her the truth.

"Jason." Zoe grabbed his hand and pulled him to a stop. "What's wrong?"

He looked up and suddenly realized how bright it was in the cabin. Their time together was quickly running out. He had to get back to his mission. He came to a decision.

"I need to tell you something important," he said, speaking quickly.

"What?" Concern shadowed her eyes.

"I'm not who you think I am." He held up his hand to stop her from interrupting. It was now or never. "I'm not a Seeker. You know my real name is Jason Parrish, but what you don't know is that I'm actually an undercover police agent working to bring down Rob Heller, or 'Brock,' as the Seekers call him."

"You're a cop." He'd expected her to be shocked or surprised, but instead, she just nodded once, tersely.

He itched to touch her, to hold her, to bridge the gulf he could feel stretching between them, but there wasn't time. He went to the sink basin and rinsed out their breakfast dishes as he tried to sum it all up quickly.

"Yes, I'm a detective. I used to work with the Humboldt County Sheriff's Office before I moved to San Francisco. It's because of my local ties here that the task force contacted my boss at the SFPD's Narcotics Division."

Zoe came over to stand beside him at the counter. "Hand me those and I'll dry them. What's the task force for?"

"To stop Heller. He's a major kingpin controlling the flow of drugs through the northern California corridor." He wiped his hands on his pants, grabbed his jacket, checked that his gun was in it, and headed for the cabin door.

"Let's go," he said.

"You're just going to drop all this on me and take off?" She followed him outside.

"I debated long and hard about telling you last night." He locked the cabin and put the key back in the old metal coffee canister.

"But you didn't."

"I kind of got distracted," he said and hurried around the side of the cabin to return the can to its hiding place.

"Will you take me to your sister's before you go after Heller?" Zoe asked when he came back.

Her words reminded him. He had to relay to Porter what he'd learned yesterday at Heller's compound about the timing of the harvest.

"Of course,' he said, slipping his burner from his jacket.

"You have a phone?" Zoe stared at him, but then answered her own question. "Of course, you're not a Seeker."

"Most of the time it's useless because of the terrible reception in the forest." He turned it on and waited for it to boot up. "We're almost at the top of the mountain here, so maybe we'll get lucky."

One bar. Not great, but better than none.

Zoe looked over his shoulder at the lit screen. "Oh my God, can we call your sister? I want to make sure Clare's OK."

He nodded as he called JoAnn. She answered on the first ring, but the reception was terrible. After getting the barest gist from JoAnn of what had happened, the phone cut out altogether. He pocketed the phone. He'd have to update Porter later.

"Is Clare there?" Zoe asked anxiously.

He shook his head. "It sounds like she and Boon stopped in, but then they left for the harvest."

"What?" She stared speechless at him in disbelief.

"Come on, we'd better get started. It's a long hike from here."

He turned and set off at a brisk pace through the forest, Zoe on his heels.

#

Why hadn't Clare and Boon followed the plan and waited for her at JoAnn's? Frustration fueled Zoe's footsteps as she rushed after Jason. *How could they be so cavalier about Clare's health and their safety?* In all likelihood, they'd run into Heller at the harvest.

She grabbed hold of a tree root that stuck out from a steep embankment above her and hoisted herself up. She was sweating and she paused to catch her breath. She pulled off her jacket, wincing as it brushed her injured arm, and tied it around her waist.

His flannel shirt smelled like him. There was so much she wanted to ask him, so much more she wanted to know. He didn't live in the back woods smoking pot and contemplating his navel all day. He lived in San Francisco like she did, and like her, he had a real job.

But if he was a cop on a mission to bust Heller, how did she and Clare fit in? Had he really been concerned about Clare's health when he first called her, or was something else going on? Like was he using them to bait Heller?

Don't be paranoid, she told herself.

She looked up and saw Jason at the top of the climb. He was checking his phone for reception again, but there must not have been any, because he put the phone away.

She summited, climbing out of the trees and onto a rocky backbone that ran along the mountainous ridgeline away from where they stood. The sun shone brilliantly on her face. Golden grass grew in the nooks and crannies between the green-colored boulders. Undulating waves of trees covered the hills that spread out below them on both sides of the tall ridge. A pair of hawks wheeled in the blue sky overhead. One uttered its distinctive, piercing cry. The air rose from the valley below, dry and warm, carrying with it the scent of trees and grass and earth.

"How beautiful!" she said.

"That's due east," Jason pointed. "Over that next ridge is where Sunrise Camp should be. We just need to get down this valley and up the other side. After what we just climbed, that shouldn't be too hard, right?" His white teeth flashed in his bearded face, his eyes narrowed against the bright sun.

She tried to imagine what he'd look like without the beard and messy hair.

"What's going on in that head of yours?" He was looking at her.

She could tell he wanted to touch her. It was there in how he moved subtly toward her, his hand leaving his side, but then, as if catching himself, he stopped, stilled the movement, and brought his hand back down. She wasn't sure if she was relieved or disappointed. He turned away and looked north.

"What is it?" she asked, following his gaze.

"Those clouds." He studied the horizon.

Streaming toward them from the north was a wide swath of high, thin clouds. A breeze kicked up and cooled the sweat on her body.

"Those are mares' tails. I don't know the scientific name. Damn, it looks like rain is on its way."

She looked at the distant clouds. They looked nothing like the puffy white cumulous that heralded the summer monsoons in Phoenix.

"They seem awfully thin to carry rain," she said.

"They're precursors, usually predicting rain in the next day or so. We're OK as far as getting to Sunrise Camp. The problem is the harvest."

"What do you mean?"

"Rain could ruin everything. Sol's going to have to start harvesting today, if he hasn't already started. I need to be there. Come on, we've gotta make tracks."

He started down fast off the other side of the rocky ridge. She hurried after him, thinking about his mission to take down Heller.

"If you're a cop, why didn't you arrest Heller last night?" she asked, as they ducked into the forest again, out of the sun and into the cool shade of the trees.

"Can you imagine him going peacefully? Even then, you got shot. I'm sorry about that."

He took her hand to keep her steady across the rocky ground. A shiver of awareness shimmered through her, feeling the warm strength of his hand enclosing hers.

"I'm OK, thanks to you," she said. Her bandaged arm didn't even hurt that much.

He let go of her hand as the grade mellowed. The release of their physical contact gave her the distance she needed to think more fully about the implications of him being a cop.

"So what about Sol and the Seekers? Are you going to bust them and Clare and Boon, too? They're all using pot and growing it."

"My target is Heller. The Seekers are growing pot illegally on federal lands, but marijuana's nothing like the heroin or the meth and the other drugs that Heller traffics in. Pot's even legal in some states. Probably here, soon, too."

She thought about how they'd found her sister last night, so high on heroin she'd have been at Heller's mercy. Thank God they'd gotten her out of there in time.

"If Clare hadn't been hanging out with the Seekers, she never would have met that creep Heller," she said.

"People in favor of legalizing pot argue that if it were legal and fully regulated, like tobacco and alcohol, then there wouldn't be such a criminal element around it."

"You believe that?"

"No, but there will always be evil. Maybe I've been in law enforcement too long, but it seems to me that for all the good people out there, there are just as many bad ones. I've seen amazing acts of courage, and empathy, and love. Like you coming up here. You didn't have to. But I've also known people too busy with their own lives and too wrapped up in their own concerns to risk what you have—your job, even your life—to come to the aid of your sister."

His compliment warmed her, but she also heard the self-criticism in his voice. "Are you talking about yourself?"

"I was too busy trying to make it in the Big City to notice what was going on back here with Tammy."

"You're being too hard on yourself."

"Let's just leave it that I admire you, OK?"

"Mutual compliments, then, since I wouldn't be here if you hadn't cared enough to notice that Clare was in trouble and call me."

They reached the bottom of the valley. It had no creek. The redwoods grew sparsely and mounds of blackberry vines and poison oak grew in places. Jason taught her how to identify them.

"'Leaves of three, let it be.' That's poison oak," he said, pointing to a bush with clusters of three shiny leaves.

Then he pointed to a different bush. "'If it's hairy, it's a berry and not scary.' That's blackberry."

"Those thorns sure look scary to me," she chuckled.

They had to deviate from their course to navigate around the thorns and the poisoned leaves. As they started up the other side of the drainage, the sunlight under the canopy suddenly dimmed and then brightened again. Clouds were moving overhead. A steady wind rustled the treetops.

"We're running out of time," Jason said.

He picked up the pace so fast that it was all she could do to keep up with him.

***

CHAPTER FIFTEEN

Wednesday Afternoon, Humboldt Forest

The weather is going to throw a monkey wrench into everything, Jason thought, glancing at the sky as Zoe and he climbed up out of the drainage.

The clouds thickened ominously overhead and visibility dimmed under the trees. The temperature began to drop. He could only imagine the chaos at the grow as the Seekers rushed to start the harvest. None of them had seen this coming. Even his Porter had said nothing to him yesterday about the weather when he'd called in from Logjammers.

Rain rarely fell in September, especially with the ongoing drought, but there was no question it was coming. He could feel the barometric pressure falling and pushed their pace as fast as he dared over the rough terrain. No way was he going to let Heller escape the bust.

They finally stepped out of the trees and onto a dirt road. He felt a surge of relief.

"Where are we?" Zoe asked, bending over to stretch out her back.

"This is the road to Sunrise Camp. We're almost there."

"How can you tell?" she asked as they started up the road.

"See how well-used it is? I've also seen aerial photographs. There aren't any other major roads between where we are now and that tall ridge we were on this morning."

He didn't mention the just-completed road to the south of the grow. Hanks had built it for bringing his logging rigs up to transport the harvest off the mountain.

"I'd kill for some water," Zoe said.

"It can't be far now," he said, realizing he was thirsty, too.

Once again, she'd surprised him. Not only with her physical ability to keep up with him, but with her attitude. She hadn't complained once during the tough, fast hike, despite scratches from blackberry bushes and scrapes from rocks.

Several bends in the road later, they came to the Sunrise Camp parking area. The Seeker vans were there, as well as Boon's VW bus and an assortment of other well-used Seeker cars. Heller's Hummer was there, and so, too were four late-model pickups and Hanks' white truck.

Jason's internal radar triggered. He stopped abruptly at the line of trees bordering the parking area.

"What is it?" Zoe asked.

"We're about to have company," he said quietly.

Quickly, he slid his gun from his pocket and tucked it into the rear waistband of his pants, keeping it hidden under his jacket. He wasn't about to have it confiscated in a pat down by one of Heller's guards.

Sure enough, as they stepped into the parking area, a man wearing camo and carrying a gun emerged from the trees nearby. With short, cropped hair and ramrod-straight posture, the guy looked ex-military, definitely not a Seeker and not someone Jason had seen before.

"Stop." The man didn't point the gun at them, but Jason caught the subtle movement of the man's finger sliding toward the trigger.

"Whoa, dude!" Jason shot his hands up in the air, relieved that Zoe followed suit and didn't try to object to the man's orders. "We're just a couple of peace, love, and understanding Seekers, man."

"Keep hands up." The man strode over, holding the gun with one hand. With the other, he cursorily patted them down, but as Jason had hoped, he didn't get anywhere near his gun.

Whose man is this?

He certainly wasn't law enforcement, but was he one of Heller's guys? Or had there been a change in power? He looked and sounded European, not Mexican cartel as Jason would have expected. Jason had an uneasy feeling they were walking into a mess. Whatever was going on, the stakes had just gone way up.

"Names," the man barked.

"Shadow, and this is Pele." Jason pointed at himself and then Zoe. "Ask Sol, he'll tell you."

The man pulled out a walkie-talkie. Keeping his gun on them, he eyed them suspiciously and verified their identities. Jason glanced at Zoe. She looked worried.

"OK." The guard waved them on.

They hurried onto the narrow footpath that led to Sunrise Camp. The moment they were out of sight of the guard, Zoe grabbed his hand and yanked him to a stop.

"Who was that?" she asked.

"Probably one of Heller's men, here to protect the harvest from poachers." He wasn't about to mention the cartels. She looked worried enough.

"Poachers?"

"There are always vultures looking to grab what they can at harvest time," he shrugged.

"How can you sound so blasé?" She stared at him. "That guy was carrying a Five-seven. That's some serious firepower."

He looked at her in surprise. "You know your weapons."

"Didn't I tell you my dad was a cop? Yes, I know guns. And I know that drugs and guns make a dangerous combination."

"That's why I want you and your sister out of here. Come on."

Minutes later, they got to Sunrise Camp. It had grown into a small city of motley-colored tarps and nylon tents, but only a few people were in sight. Jason brushed back his hair and assumed his laid-back persona as he walked over to Rabbit and her friend who were seated at a card table chopping vegetables.

"Hey, Rabbit, how's it going?" He adopted the slow, drawn-out way of speaking used by the Seekers.

"Good to see you, Shadow." Rabbit's long, beaded dreadlocks tinkled as she jerked her head nervously, her eyes flitting from him back to her work. "We were wondering where you and Pele got to." She darted a glance at Zoe, who was scooping water from a big bucket with a plastic cup.

"We had to make a detour, but we're here, now. It's all good."

Zoe came over and handed him a cup of water.

"Do you know where my sister is?" she asked Rabbit.

"Probably up harvesting with the others. Everything's crazy busy now, what with the rain coming."

"Hectic, yeah. Let's go help," he said to Zoe.

#

When they reached the garden, Zoe looked around in surprise. In the two days since she'd been there, the pot plants had grown even taller, towering overhead like small trees. The place bustled with activity as the harvest began. Some Seekers continued to chant at the plants, others were cutting them down, and in the newly created spaces made by the absence of the plants, other Seekers nailed together rudimentary structures of lumber that they then covered with plastic sheeting.

Zoe scanned the crowds, looking for her sister. She felt a rush of relief. Inside one of the huts, she spotted Clare working beside Boon. Clare sat cross-legged on the ground, trimming leaves off a huge, bushy pot plant.

Zoe hurried over. "I'm so glad you're OK!"

Clare pushed the plant off her lap. Boon took her hand and helped her up. She held out her arms to Zoe, tears in her eyes.

"Praise be to Gaia," she said, trying to hug Zoe.

Zoe pushed aside Clare's hands. "Why didn't you follow the plan? You were supposed to wait for me at JoAnn's."

"We told her where we went," Clare said defensively, "but the harvest is what matters right now."

"You wanna help?" Boon interjected. "Take a plant and clip it, like this."

He held up a trimmed pot plant and used a clothespin to attach it to one of the lines strung up inside the wooden hut. He clipped it so that it hung downwards without its stem or big bud touching any of the others crowding together inside the hut. He tried to hand a plant to Zoe.

"I didn't come all this way to help harvest a bunch of pot." She put her hands on her hips and scowled down at her sister. "I came to help you."

Clare had resumed trimming the pot. "I appreciate that you care, Sis, but the rain could ruin everything. Don't worry. When the harvest is over, Boon's promised he'll take me to see the doc in Garberville." Clare smiled again at Boon, who smiled back. They were quite obviously in love.

Zoe looked more closely at her sister. Clare still looked terribly pale, with dark circles under her eyes, but she seemed fueled by a manic energy, like the last flare-up before collapse. Foreboding slithered through Zoe.

"What about Heller—Brock? He could show up at any moment. You're not safe. None of us are safe," she added in a much softer voice as one of the guards sauntered by, a handgun attached to a holster on his belt, his eyes moving over them.

Clare followed her gaze. "Sol says we need these men to keep us safe from the bad people who want to steal our plants."

Zoe looked apprehensively at the guards, the guns, and all the pot plants that the people were frantically harvesting. The heavy, gathering clouds added to the dangerous atmosphere. The trees on all sides felt like walls, trapping everyone in the clearing under the flat gray lid of sky.

She scanned the area for Jason, but he'd disappeared. Several hulking man lurched into the clearing, carrying heavy loads of lumber and supplies. She recognized the biggest and burliest of them. It was Derrick Hanks. He stomped over to Sol who was working near the hut where she stood.

"We need more space for the drying huts, but these fucking trees are in our way." Hanks' voice rose above everything else going on, clearly audible as he yelled at Sol.

He swung a chainsaw up to waist height and cranked it on, revving it a few times aggressively, the roar of the machine violently deafening. He moved toward the first line of trees at the edge of the clearing, but Sol moved quicker, stepping between him and the trees. He spread his arms out, his body a human shield between the chainsaw and the trees. Hanks killed the chainsaw, but he still held it up like a weapon, threatening. He fumed with anger.

"Look at the fucking sky!" he shouted. "The rain's coming. We've only got a few hours to get all this shit under cover. I can get these trees cleared in ten minutes, enough to make room for at least three more huts, otherwise you're gonna lose a lot of plants and a lot of fucking money."

Sol shook his head. "It is not about the money. These trees are sacred and holy. They are what makes this soil rich and fertile and what gives our plants their wholesome power. They hold an ancient wisdom. They were here long before we ever were and will be here long after us. Please don't waste any more energy in anger, but help us build what drying huts we can before the rain."

For an instant, it looked like Hanks was going to attack Sol with the chainsaw, his anger rampantly palpable on his red, beefy face. Sol kept his arms outstretched, as if waiting to embrace Hanks. He seemed completely unaffected by Hanks' rage. Zoe held her breath as the moment stretched between the two men.

Then, the fight abruptly went out of Hanks. His stance relaxed and he lowered the chainsaw. Sol patted him on the shoulder.

She watched the two men walk away together, surprised to feel a newfound respect for Sol. His calm, compassionate manner and refusal to engage Hanks' anger had defused the burly guy and rendered him harmless.

But nonviolence could only accomplish so much. She turned and looked back at her sister and Boon and all the other Seekers. The situation was far from harmless, because really they were all just sitting ducks, surrounded by millions of dollars of drugs that anyone with bigger and more numerous guns could come and take. She looked around again for Jason. Where was he?

#

Jason watched Zoe go to her sister, and then, when the guards weren't looking, he melted into the trees. He checked his burner and confirmed he still had no reception. He needed his sat phone. It was way past time to check in with Porter.

He moved stealthily through the forest to the ridge above the grow, where he'd hidden his operations stash, his satellite phone, additional rounds of ammo, and his IDs. He hurried to the outcrop of serpentine, where no trees grew in the harsh alkaline soil. The vein of greenish rock ran the rest of the way up the ridge to the distant summit, creating a rocky open space under the cloudy sky.

He started pulling away the rocks hiding his stash when he suddenly noticed the stillness of the afternoon around him. No breeze rustled the trees or the grass. The small sounds of the land had stopped, as if all the animals had taken cover. He smelled no rain on the air, but it felt like a storm was brewing. Something about it made him uneasy.

He felt too exposed in the open. He grabbed the sat phone and the cartridges of ammo and climbed down off the ridge closer to the protection of the trees before calling his boss.

"Porter, it's Jason," he said, using his shoulder to hold the phone against his ear as he loaded his gun with a new cartridge.

"About fucking time. No rain yet?"

"Why didn't warn me about the weather?"

"The front took us all by surprise. It was supposed to track north to Oregon."

"No shit. The harvest is in full swing. What's the timeline to bust Heller?"

"Change of plans, Parrish. We're coordinating with the DEA."

"What? Last I heard, you said you'd be damned before you'd work with the Feds."

"That's yesterday's news. Turns out your intel about the DEA moving in was right. They're concerned about cartel infiltration of the Emerald Triangle as well as the whole northern California corridor. We've teamed up with them, but we're on their timeline now."

"What does that mean?"

"I'm en route with our team now. We just got off the Redwood Highway and should be there within the hour. The DEA is setting up an operations command post on that logging road south of the grow."

"Already? But Heller's not currently on site."

"Doesn't matter at this point."

"I thought the whole reason for this task force was to get a conviction against Heller." The bastard couldn't walk, not now, especially not after what he almost did to Zoe's sister.

"Turns out the DEA has bigger fish to fry. Heller's just a bit player in the bigger cartel game."

"That must explain all the new men and weaponry I'm seeing. You should let everyone know there are guards staked everywhere, some armed with FN Five-sevens."

"Fuck, just what we need, goddamned cartel guys with fancy guns."

"I've gotta go. See you soon." Jason hung up.

As he raced downhill through the trees, he thought of Zoe, her sister, and all the other unarmed people at the harvest who could so easily get caught in the crossfire. The DEA didn't always concern themselves with the welfare of innocent bystanders. Heller's men and the cartel dudes would undoubtedly care even less.

When he reached the harvest, a flash of light caught his eye. He looked westward. The overcast sky had thickened into a leaden bank of clouds, underneath so dark it looked like night. A distant rumble sounded across the mountaintops. For a moment, the frenzy of the harvest stopped. The trimmers stopped trimming, the harvesters stopped harvesting, and even the guards slowed their patrol of the area.

Damn, the storm's getting closer, Jason thought as more lightning flashed, followed by echoing thunder.

He scanned the clearing and spotted Zoe with her sister and Boon under one of the drying huts. He had to warn her about what was going down. He started forward, but a beardless guard with a crew cut noticed him and approached.

"Get to work," the man grunted, his accent thick and foreign.

"Dude, I had to take care of nature's urges," Jason shrugged and acted nonchalant as he walked past the guard toward Zoe.

Her face lit up when she saw him. "Where did you go?"

"Pele, sweetheart, give me a hug."

He hauled her against him, wrapping his arms around her and pressing their bodies together all the way down. She sighed and wrapped her hands around his shoulders.

God, she felt good.

He breathed in the scent of her. There wasn't time for this, but he couldn't resist. For a long moment, he held her. Then, he put his mouth to her ear.

"This is the only way we can talk without being overheard," he whispered.

"Did you talk to your boss?"

"Yes, you've got to get out of here."

"I won't go without my sister, but she won't leave, at least not until the plants are under the drying huts."

"That may be too late," Jason said, frustration coursing through him.

"Excuse me." Clarity came up.

Jason dropped his arms and stepped back from Zoe. Clarity moved between the two of them and pointedly turned her back on him.

"Can I talk to you?" she said to Zoe.

"Sure." Zoe glanced at him over Clarity's shoulder and gave a slight shrug.

"Go to Sunrise Camp," he called after them as they walked away from the drying hut to a denuded area of the clearing. A Seeker came up and handed him a pair of scissors.

"Dude, didn't you hear that thunder? The rain'll be here any second." The guy thrust an enormous marijuana plant at him, its branches loaded down with huge hairy buds, the thing reeking with its overpowering odor.

#

Zoe followed Clare away from Jason. They stood on the uneven, churned-up earth where the pot plants had been cut down. Clare turned around and put her hands on her hips.

She frowned at Zoe, her blue eyes sharp. "So, you and Shadow, when did that happen?"

"What?" Zoe couldn't believe Clare would pick a time like this to discuss her love life. She gave a little laugh. "You don't have to look so concerned. "

"I am, Sis. He's not your type. Besides, you don't do flings, or at least you didn't used to." Clare's voice faltered, a combination of uncertainty and fatigue lacing it. She dropped her hands from her hips and lowered herself to sit cross-legged on the ground.

"You OK?" Zoe crouched beside her.

"Just tired." Clare's troubled blue eyes met hers. "You didn't answer my question."

"He just gave me a hug, that's all."

"You don't do hugs, Sis. You're not the hugging type."

"When did you become Miss Judgmental, huh? Where's all the love and acceptance you're always going on about?"

She hadn't meant to go on the attack, not with her sister so weak and tired, but she couldn't help the anger bubbling up. It was just like Clare to focus on the irrelevant, when she should be concerned about getting herself medical attention. Besides, Zoe didn't want to think about Jason and what had happened between them. Maybe later, when she was back in her own life, but right now it was cope-and-deal time, and they had to get out of there before the police showed up.

Clare touched her gently on her bent knee. "I do love you and that's why I'm worried."

Zoe frowned. "Are you're saying there's something wrong with Jason?"

"You mean Shadow? Of course not, he's a great guy, but I'm not sure you're thinking clearly right now."

"What?"

"Hang on, I'm not finished." Clare held up a hand to stop her from interrupting. "I know how hard you've been trying to build a life for yourself, with your career, your car, your apartment in San Francisco, all those civilized things, but being out here, so close to nature and bare survival, it's put you in an emotionally vulnerable place."

"Are you kidding me?" Zoe jumped to her feet in outrage. "I know exactly what I'm doing!" But then she caught sight of the busy clearing and wondered if that was really true.

When she'd set out to find Clare, she'd had no idea what kind of illegal operation she was walking into. This was way beyond anything she could have imagined. She caught sight of Jason. He and Boon were building another drying hut. She watched him expertly handle a hammer, pounding in nails to join two pieces of wood. If she hadn't known he was a cop, she would've had no idea he wasn't a full-fledged Seeker like Boon and the others.

"Sis." Clare got up and stood beside her. She noticed where Zoe was looking. "You haven't been with many men. Not surprising after what happened with Mike."

She turned and glared at Clare. "That was a *very* long time ago. I thought I made it clear that we would *never* speak of that jerk again."

Jerk was a complete understatement. Mike had been a total loser slimeball. He'd been the attorney overseeing their parents' meager estate after the car crash. She'd been in college and he'd seemed so successful and dashing, an older man who could provide support and comfort after losing her parents. She'd practically thrown herself into his arms. What a naive fool! She'd never make that mistake again.

She'd had enough of this ridiculous conversation!

"I'm *not* having a fling with Shadow," she said with finality. She ruthlessly quashed her guilt for lying to her sister. "Let's stay focused on the real issue here. Look at you! You're so weak it's all you can do to stay standing. We need to get you to a doctor immediately. Besides, the weather's about to turn ugly. It feels electric, like before the storms we used to get back home."

She looked up at the dark, menacing sky and then at her sister again.

"'Home'?" A sad smile played across Clare's face. "The one you're talking about disappeared when mom and dad died. This is my home now."

A booming roar sounded over the mountaintops, but unlike thunder, it grew steadily louder, changing frequency as it came closer.

"It's the cops!" someone shouted across the clearing.

The armed guards looked upwards, their rifles pointed at the sky. Within moments, the clearing was filled with the chopping sound of an approaching helicopter.

***

CHAPTER SIXTEEN

Wednesday Mid-Afternoon, Humboldt Forest

Jason looked up at the helicopter flying under the dark, scudding clouds.

That's not ours, he thought. Their task force only had one helicopter, and this wasn't it, and it was too large and way too pricey-looking to be local county law enforcement. The DEA must be doing the aerial recon before launching their offensive.

The chopper circled overhead once and then disappeared over the trees. Jason checked for Zoe and Clarity. Wisely, Zoe had moved her sister out of the open and over to the tree line.

"Can I talk to you a minute?" he said to Boon who was helping him construct one of the drying huts.

"What's up?"

"Can you help Pele get Clarity out of here?"

"Why?"

"I'm pretty sure that helicopter was the DEA. Things could get real ugly, real soon, if they're planning a bust."

"We need to tell Sol!" Boon looked around the

clearing for the Seeker leader.

"I'll do that," Jason said.

He looked for Sol but couldn't locate him among all the other people and drying huts. Instead, he spotted Heller arguing with a foreign-looking man in a track suit with close-cropped hair and a pasty complexion. The man was gesticulating emphatically as he spoke. The guy had to be cartel. Why were they arguing? It couldn't be good.

"We can't abandon everybody," Boon said, "not if the DEA's coming."

"Think, Boon," Jason said, talking quickly. "You see all those guys with guns, right? Don't kid yourself about why they're here. They're not going to defend or help us. They're here to take the harvest, either from us or from anyone else who might horn in on it. You don't want Clarity caught in the crossfire, right?"

Boon studied him. It was obvious he was weighing what Jason had told him and considering the ramifications.

After a moment, he said, "OK, I'll do what I can, though I don't think Clarity's going to listen. She's got strong opinions."

"So does her sister," Jason grinned.

"Where should we go?"

"Sunrise Camp. It's going to start raining any minute. You can take shelter in the tents."

Boon nodded and headed for the two sisters. Jason needed to hear what Heller and the cartel guy were talking about. He took his hammer and went over to where some other Seekers were erecting another drying hut just a few feet from the two men.

#

Zoe flinched as lightning stabbed the sky over the harvest, followed by a crash of thunder that echoed through the trees all around where she and Clare stood. Another lightning bolt struck. She grabbed Clare's hand.

"Come on!" she shouted and pulled Clare after her as the electrical storm hit.

Lightning flashed, and then again, so close that the ground rocked under them as the thunder boomed. Another flash, but not a drop of rain fell.

Zoe tried to pull Clare deeper into the forest, but Clare fell to the ground, her hands pressed against her ears, her eyes squeezed shut. Zoe crouched and put her arm around her sister. She'd forgotten how terrified Clare was of thunderstorms.

Unlike the summer thunderstorms they were used to in the desert, this storm seemed much bigger than a single cell, and it stuck right on top of them, the lightning flashes so continual that the forest pulsed as if lit by some surreal strobe light.

Boon appeared through the trees. He dropped to his knees and yelled something to Zoe, but she couldn't hear him over the thunder booming all around them. He took her place by her sister's side.

She rocked back on her heels and yelled at Boon. "I'm going to get Shadow. Stay here and don't move!"

Boon said something in reply, but she couldn't hear him over the roaring thunder. He could tell her later. Last she'd seen, Jason had been in the clearing working on one of the drying huts. She raced back through the trees to the clearing.

The place was in chaos. Seekers ran every which way in the whipping wind, trying to get control of the harvest, but the wind toppled drying huts and ripped the tarps off. The carefully hung pot plants flapped wildly and many fell to the ground, crushed under the running feet of Seekers. Other plants were being rescued by other Seekers, hurrying to pick up as many as they could. Guards gestured vehemently with guns at each other. Were any of them the law enforcement that Jason said would be showing up? She couldn't tell who was who. They all looked equally dangerous.

The crack of gunshot pierced through the booming thunder. As Zoe dropped to the ground, she saw a man buckle at the edge of the clearing, not ten feet from where she lay. It was Derrick Hanks. He crumpled to his knees, dropping his gun and grabbing his belly. She put her head down, inhaling the rich, pungent smell of the earth as a bunch of loose pot leaves brushed against her cheek. Several more gunshots followed. She prayed Jason was somewhere safe and that her sister and Boon had stayed in the cover of the trees.

Suddenly, lightning exploded directly overhead, followed instantaneously by booming thunder and the acrid smell of ozone. A terrific crack sounded almost directly above her and she realized a tree must have been struck, but she was still blinded by the lightning. Instinctively, she rolled away as fast as she could, feeling the ground shake as the tree split apart and fell. There was the sound of impact and something scratched across her face. She blinked rapidly until her vision cleared. A huge branch had smashed down, scattering splinters of shattered wood everywhere. The needles on one of the smaller branches started to smoke. In horror, she watched as a single yellow flame curled upwards and then was spurred on by the gusting wind into a crackling fire. The flames jumped to a bush, just five feet from where she lay.

What should she do? She could get up and possibly be

hit by gunfire, or she could stay and be roasted alive as the flames grew into a raging forest fire. If only it would start to rain!

It was hard to think with the lightning and thunder, more gunshots, the wind blowing, and now the Seekers were screaming. Several seemed to have been shot and Sol and Luna were there, running between the fallen people.

From where Zoe lay, she could see that the fire had already grown into a wall of flaming bushes, spurred on by the howling wind. The fire line was moving away from her through the trees toward the spot where she'd left Clare and Boon.

Where are you, Jason?

Lightning ripped the sky again. She risked craning her head upward and looked desperately for him, but there were too many people milling around, and now smoke was beginning to fill the air, adding to the chaos. Over the roar of the thunder, she heard the crack of more gunshot.

She was a sitting duck if she stayed lying there on the ground. She had to find Clare and get them both out of there. Summoning her courage, she launched herself to her feet, grit her teeth against any sudden bullet impacts, and raced back into the trees.

#

The moment the lightning storm cut loose, Jason sprinted into the forest in the opposite direction from where Boon had gone after Zoe and Clare. He had to tell Porter what he'd learned from Heller's argument with the cartel guy.

He headed for the road Hanks had built down the mountain on the south side of the grow, descending through the trees. A gun fired somewhere behind him up the hill, its sharp, man-made sound an echo of the thunder booming all around. The first gunshot was followed by more rounds, from different guns. He smelled smoke on the wind.

Had the bust already started? Or had the ugly situation between Heller's men and the cartel turned deadly? He hoped to God that Zoe, her sister, and Boon had gotten safely to Sunrise Camp, but that was out of his hands now.

He reached the trees bordering the logging road and took stock of the situation in the dim light that was frequently punctuated by lightning flashes. Down the road from where he hid, several men in DEA jackets were handcuffing a group of Heller's men beside a logging truck rigged with a shipping container.

The bust had begun.

He didn't see his boss, but he recognized one of the guys in uniform. He stepped out onto the road and kept his hands up as he walked down the road to the men.

"Hey there, Barker," he called out, "it's me, Parrish."

Barker looked up, studied him for a moment, and then broke into a grin. "Like the hairdo. You look like a hillbilly."

"That's the idea. Where's Porter?"

"Down there," Barker said, pointing farther downhill. "Come with me and my buddy here."

Barker pushed the handcuffed man down the road. Jason followed them to a line of SUVs and prisoner transport vans. The second SUV was serving as the command center. Porter was there along with another two men Jason didn't recognize. One was monitoring communications while the tall guy had to be the operations lead, the way he was talking to Porter, who was nodding and acting deferential. Jason stepped forward.

"Parrish! Good." Porter uncharacteristically held off with the swear words as he addressed the tall man standing beside him. "This is my operative, Jason Parrish. He's the one who's been undercover with the Seekers."

The tall man gave Jason the once-over but looked underwhelmed. Jason instantly disliked him and his condescending attitude. He turned to his boss.

"These cartel guys aren't Mexican," he said to Porter.

"The Balkans. We already know about them," the tall man interjected and then turned away.

"Let the Feds worry about the cartel, Parrish," Porter said quietly. "You focus on Heller. Don't let him get away. I'll do what I can on this end, but get back up to the harvest, ASAP." Porter grabbed a Colt semi-automatic from the SUV and pressed it into Jason's hands.

"You're gonna need this. Now get the fuck out of here!"

Jason wasn't about to turn down the extra firepower. He took the gun and sprinted back up the mountain into the blowing wind and smoke.

#

A few fat raindrops hit her face as Zoe raced from tree to tree looking for Clare and Boon. The wind blew in gusts filled with clouds of choking, blinding smoke. She wiped her stinging eyes with the back of her hand as she moved cautiously from tree to tree. She hadn't seen a soul since reentering the forest, but no way did she want to encounter one of those armed men. Maybe they were keeping everyone hostage at the clearing, or maybe

Jason's task force had moved in. Another gunshot sounded, echoing off the trees.

"Clare!" She risked calling for her sister, but then doubled over, coughing from the smoke.

She pulled the hem of Jason's flannel shirt up and did her best to cover her mouth and nose as she moved forward. The forest brightened ominously. In the flickering light, she recognized the huge stump of the old tree where she'd left her sister with Boon. Just beyond it, the forest fire rose up, a wall of flames. There was no way they waited for her there. They must have left for Sunrise Camp.

A violent gust of wind caused a plume of white-hot flame to shoot up into the crown of a pine tree. She turned and ran from the raging inferno, retreating back to the line of trees bordering the clearing. Circling the area, she raced as fast as she could through the smoke and encroaching darkness of night. She made it to the foot trail to Sunrise Camp just as the pelting rain gave way to a torrential downpour, streaming water into her eyes and slowing her pace.

She cursed, wiping water from her eyes with both hands as she stumbled down the trail. A few hundred yards onward, she spotted someone ahead. She peered through the rain at the person, who had long blond hair that hung lank and wet with rain. She heaved a sigh of relief.

"Clare!" She called out.

Clare turned, Boon at her side. They both smiled at her.

"Thank all the stars in heaven," Clare said. "Did you find Shadow?"

"No." She tamped down her fear. Jason was a professional. She had to trust that he could take care of himself.

"Let's get to Sunrise Camp and out of this rain," Boon said, turning to lead the way down the trail.

Zoe followed her sister, who seemed shrunken, her arms wrapped tightly around herself, her shoulders hunched under the downpour.

By the time they reached Sunrise Camp, the storm had wrecked the place, flooding everything with water, and many of the tents looked like they'd taken a serious beating with the canvas structures collapsed in places. Several of the plastic tarps hung in strips, their plastic sheeting shredded by the wind. No one appeared to be around, at least not outside the tents.

Boon led them to a small nylon tent that had managed to withstand the wind. It stood on a slight rise above the flooded ground, so it wasn't flooded. He hunkered down and pulled back the tent flaps for Clare before following her inside. Zoe poked her head in. Boon was helping Clare out of her wet jacket. The air inside felt wonderfully warm and dry.

"Are those dry?" She spoke loudly over the rain pounding against the tent and gestured to the blankets on the floor.

Clare fingered the fabric and nodded as Boon wrapped one around her and then pulled her against him. She closed her eyes.

"I'll see if I can find some food," Zoe said. Calories would help warm them up.

"Thanks," Boon yelled. "Check the plastic bins by the tables."

Zoe closed the tent flaps and headed across the camp in the pouring rain to the tables. She wiped more rainwater from her eyes and considered pulling the bins out from under the table so she could more easily look inside, but if she did that, whatever was inside would get drenched. Instead, she leaned over and tried to pry open one of the lids. She had just managed to lift the lid when someone grabbed the back of her leather jacket.

"Well, well, well, if it isn't my ticket out of here." A man's voice sounded behind her.

He hauled her up, his grip on her jacket pulling her hair. She ignored the pain and twisted around to identify the man. It was Heller, his expression flat like the snake he was. The hard, unforgiving steel of a gun poked her in the ribs.

***

CHAPTER SEVENTEEN

Wednesday Late Afternoon, Humboldt Forest

By the time Jason got back to the clearing, he discovered the source of the smoke. Whether caused by lightning or manmade, a growing forest fire was being stoked by the howling west wind. Sparks flew through the air, igniting everything they touched. Several drying huts burned, and marijuana smoke and toxic black clouds from the melting plastic blew overhead. Groups of people were silhouetted against the fiery backdrop. The Seekers were easily identifiable with their long hair and lack of firepower, standing helplessly by while law enforcement and the cartel, who were heavily armed and dressed in paramilitary outfits, faced off. Some kind of standoff was in the making.

Fat raindrops struck his face as he crouched and scanned the clearing, looking for Zoe. He saw no sign of her, or Clarity, or Heller, either. Someone approached from the left and he spun around, gun drawn.

"Parrish?" It was a member of the task force.

He lowered his weapon. "How's it going?"

"So far, so good, though the weather's not helping."

No sooner had the words left the man's mouth when the light rain gave way to a torrential downpour.

"You've gotta be kidding me!" the man groaned.

"At least it'll help put out the fire." Jason shook out his mane of hair, sending water flying. "Has Heller been apprehended?"

"Not that I've heard."

A DEA agent herded a group of bedraggled Seekers past Jason toward Hanks' logging road. Sol and Luna were there. Sol's eyes met his, a deep sadness in them. Jason couldn't tell if Sol's red eyes came from tears, the rain, or the smoke, but Sol had to be devastated, considering the marijuana he'd labored over for so long and with so much care was now completely destroyed.

"I'm with the task force," Jason said to the DEA agent, who was scowling suspiciously at him. "I need to ask this man a few questions. It's important."

"Make it quick."

Jason turned to Sol. "Have you seen Clarity or Pele?"

Sol looked down at the gun in Jason's hand. "I knew you hid shadows, but I thought they were only of your past. You lied to us about who you are." Sol's expression shifted from sadness to weariness as he wiped rainwater from his face. He looked old.

"I'm sorry, Sol, but it was never about the Seekers. My target has always been Heller—Brock. Have you seen him?"

Sol shook his head, "Not recently."

Unease filled Jason. Had Heller headed for Sunrise Camp? If so, there was the very real and terrible possibility that they were all together.

"Gotta get a move on," the DEA agent said to Jason and nudged Sol and the group down the road toward the waiting transport vans.

Jason pivoted and broke into a run, ignoring the pouring rain that streamed down and made it hard to see. He raced back across the clearing to the foot trail leading to Sunrise Camp as fast as he could.

#

Heller's gun prodded Zoe unpleasantly in the ribs. She glared at him in the downpour.

"What do you mean, I'm your ticket out of here?" she demanded, hoping Clare and Boon would stay safely hidden in the tent. No way was she going to let Heller get his hands on her sister again.

"Parrish won't risk hurting you."

Heller spoke with such certainty. How did he know what Jason felt for her? She wasn't even sure she knew what he really felt.

"What do you mean?"

"Once a cop, always a cop, right?"

She reached up to wipe the rainwater out of her eyes, but Heller used his grip on her jacket collar to shake her violently, reminding her again of his brutal strength.

"Don't do anything stupid, bitch." He prodded her again with the gun. "Move."

With his other hand a relentless vise on her collar, he propelled her forward, marching her away from the picnic table and the tents and toward the trail to the parking lot. The deluge had turned the trail spongy, and as they descended his hand on her collar jerked her hair painfully.

"Stop pulling my hair!" she snapped and tried to reach up to the back of her head.

"Do that and die." He jabbed the gun meaningfully against her.

"OK, I get the message," she said, lowering her hand.

"But can you please stop?"

He ignored her request and shoved her forward as the rain abruptly stopped.

He hauled her up short just before they reached the end of the trail. Releasing her collar, he pushed her hard against a tree with one hand, positioning her so she couldn't see the parking lot. He swung the gun away from her and fired. The gunshot was deafening, but she ignored her ringing ears and strained forward to see.

Had he shot Jason?

A man she didn't recognize clung to the side of Heller's black Hummer. As she watched, the man fell to the ground.

"You killed that man!" she exclaimed in horror.

Icy adrenaline jolted through her. No way was Heller going to let her go, not now that she was a murder witness. He seized her by the collar again and pushed the gun against her.

"Move," he said, forcing her into the open.

She looked around desperately for help, but there was only that one man, who now lay dead on the ground beside the Hummer. The clouds scudded off eastward on the wind. The sun had set, and the sky glowed with a pearly luminescence she'd have found beautiful if she wasn't afraid for her life.

Her brain raced through possible escape scenarios as Heller marched her across the parking area to his vehicle. She could try to get clear of him before they got into the Hummer, or she could wait until after they were inside. She'd seen how he'd shot that man in cold blood. He could too easily kill her if she tried anything now, but once they were inside the Hummer, the game would change. The drive down the mountain would demand both his hands to negotiate the rough road. He'd be distracted, a good time to make her move, unless he tied her up.

"Hands up." Heller shoved her forward so that her hands were braced on the passenger side of the Hummer. "Don't move."

While Heller jingled a pair of keys from his pocket and unlocked the door, she glanced over her shoulder at the dead man lying just a few feet away. Heller had shot him in the head. She looked away from the grisly sight, but then her eyes landed on the man's gun. It had slid under the Hummer and lay within inches of her left foot. She felt a surge of hope. Maybe she could get her hands on it, but how? She needed to stall him.

"Your escape plan isn't going to work," she said as he swung open the front passenger door.

Distant engines fired up.

"You hear that?" she said, talking fast. "The police are coming. Now's your chance. Get out of here and I'll stall them so you can get a head start!"

"Shut up, bitch," Heller said. He transferred the gun to his left hand so he could use his right to hoist himself up onto the Hummer's running board. He kept his eyes and gun pointed at her. "Don't try anything stupid."

She waited for the moment to make her move. Maybe it was stupid to go for the dead man's gun, but with the police coming, there was no way she wanted to be trapped inside the Hummer with Heller. Very likely she'd be caught in the crossfire.

Heller reached inside the Hummer with his right arm, his eyes and gun still trained on her. She heard him pop open the glove compartment and grope around in it. She had no idea what he was searching for, but the instant he looked away from her to glance inside the compartment, she knew it was now or never.

She dropped to her knees and grabbed the dead man's gun. Her right index finger settled over the trigger as she swung it up toward Heller.

"You are a stupid bitch, aren't you?" Heller dangled a pair of handcuffs in his right hand, his gun in his left. "What you gonna do, try and shoot me, 'cause I'll shoot you first."

For a long second, they stared at each other. A gunshot pierced their standoff.

"Zoe, run!" A man shouted from the trees, his gun pointed skyward.

Jason!

#

Jason jumped behind the cover of the redwood tree and dropped to his knees as Heller fired. The bullet went wide. He swung around the tree and returned fire. Heller launched himself backwards through the Hummer's open passenger side door, yanking it closed behind him, but not before Jason heard Heller's grunt of pain.

Jason felt an instant's satisfaction at landing a shot, but then felt uneasy. Where was Zoe? She'd disappeared behind the Hummer when he'd fired the first shot skyward.

He scanned the vicinity for any sign of her, but then the Hummer's passenger side window exploded. Another bullet whizzed by, so close it spit bark at him. He dove back behind the tree.

Zoe came running through the trees to his right, carrying a gun. She reached him just as another bullet cracked the bark of the redwood tree several feet above their heads. He grabbed her with his free arm and pulled her completely behind the broad redwood trunk.

"What the hell are you doing? You could've been shot!" Anger warred with concern as he hugged her close.

"Heller was too focused on you to pay attention to where I was." Zoe gave him a light peck on the cheek. "Thanks for rescuing me."

"Anytime, but," he tilted her chin up with his free hand and gave her a quick hard kiss on the mouth, "you can thank me properly after we get Heller."

"Promise?" she grinned.

The Hummer's powerful engine roared to life.

"We can't let him get away!" She pulled out of his arms.

"We won't. Where did that come from?" He looked at the gun in her hands.

"The dead guy." She pointed.

"Good thinking. Any rounds in it?"

"Five."

"Excellent." He caught her eye. "Maybe when this is all over, you can tell me more about your dad and how you learned so much about guns."

She nodded.

They proceeded cautiously out from behind the tree and into the parking area, but the Hummer was already moving, heading for the road out of there.

"I'll take the left tire, you take the right," he said, stopping to take aim.

The left rear tire popped. Simultaneously, the right rear tire popped.

"Great shot!" he said, surprised. She'd taken out the tire on her first try. He gave her a thumb's up.

The Hummer's rear end sagged, banging over the rocky ground as it left the parking area and dragged heavily down the dirt road. Heller wasn't going to get far.

"Take the passenger side. I'll take the driver side," he

said, glancing at Zoe. She held her gun professionally, at the ready.

"You're not going to kill him, right?" She met his gaze.

"I won't kill him if I don't have to."

"That doesn't reassure me."

"Don't worry, my plan is to arrest him. Let's go!"

As they ran toward the Hummer, its driver side door swung open and Heller jumped out of the moving vehicle. Jason took a shot, but from the way Heller dashed into the trees, he knew he'd missed.

He cursed as he ran after Heller into the forest. They'd raced together on the track team in high school, but Heller had held the school record for sprints. Maybe all the muscle he'd put on over the years would slow him down.

Jason picked up his pace to keep Heller in sight, but the trees and bushes created all kinds of obstacles. The wet branches slapped against him and twilight dimmed the forest. He heard Zoe on his tail.

She runs like a deer, he thought as he swerved around a tree.

He pushed even faster as Heller ploughed ahead, hurdling bushes and weaving in and out of the closely packed trees, trying to lose them.

Suddenly, the forest opened into a grassy glade.

Heller realized his mistake too late. He tried to dash back into the trees, but Jason and Zoe were closing in. Jason took a shot and caught Heller in the leg. Heller fell forward, crying out, but then rolled onto his stomach, turned, and opened fire.

"Down!" Jason whirled and grabbed Zoe, pulling her down beside him onto the tall, wet grass, which provided only meager cover as bullets flew by way too close for comfort.

Heller stopped shooting and reloaded his gun.

"Drop your weapon, Heller!" Jason yelled.

"You're outgunned," Zoe added and he glanced over at her. She lay like he did, with her gun arm braced over her other arm. Her eyes were trained on Heller with laser-like focus.

"Give up, Heller," Jason called out. "I've already shot you twice. Cut your losses while you can."

"I'm going to fucking kill you!" Heller screamed with the fury of a trapped animal.

He rose to his knees and began shooting wildly at them. They returned fire. Heller's body jerked and then fell, but this time, he lay unmoving on the ground. Jason's ears rang in the echoing silence.

"Did we kill him?" Zoe whispered.

"I don't know. He may be down, but he could still be dangerous." Jason kept his gun on Heller as he got up from the grass. "Stay behind me."

He moved cautiously to Heller, who lay on his stomach, the gun still clutched in his hand. His body was splayed across the ground at an unnatural angle and dark blood seeped from several points on his arms and legs.

"Keep me covered," Jason said quietly over his shoulder to Zoe.

He dropped to one knee and pried the gun from Heller's unmoving fingers. He slid it into his jacket pocket and checked Heller's carotid for a pulse. A mix of emotions moved through him as he felt the telltale throb.

"He's not dead," he said.

He rolled Heller over and fastened a pair of handcuffs to his wrists. Zoe stood beside him, watching.

"Do you wish he were?" she asked.

"It'd be simpler."

"At least he'll stand trial," she said.

"You bet."

He hoisted Heller over his shoulder in a fireman's carry and started back for the parking area. The guy was heavy, a pile of dead-weight muscle. Zoe followed him through the gathering darkness. The DEA and task force convoy inched its way into view, their headlights bouncing off trees and illuminating the parking area.

Jason led the way to the first approaching vehicle, a large 4x4 van. It stopped and the tinted driver side window lowered. An unfamiliar man looked suspiciously at them. Jason lifted his hand off Heller's thigh and waved.

"Parrish—task force operative," he added when his name didn't register with the DEA agent. "We bagged Rob Heller." He patted the back of Heller's thigh, where it draped over his shoulder.

"We thought he got away." The man dropped his guarded expression, spoke into his headset, and then said to Jason, "Knock on the back panel. They'll take Heller."

"Help! We need help!" Someone called out from the dark forest behind them.

"Clare!" Zoe cried.

Jason shifted Heller's weight and turned around to look. Zoe ran back to where Boon came out of the forest with Clarity in his arms. The glare of the headlights made them look ghostly white.

#

Fear shot through Zoe as she ran to her sister in Boon's arms. Clare's head rested against his shoulder. Her eyes were closed, and her face was so pale it seemed to blend into her blond hair. She was bundled in a thick blanket. One white hand clutched it together under her neck. Her eyes fluttered open when Zoe reached them.

"Hey Sis." Clare's teeth clenched and her jaw stood out in sharp relief, as if she were in pain.

"What happened?" Zoe asked.

Boon spoke up. "We were in the tent talking when her legs started to cramp so bad she started to scream. And then she tried to throw up, but she hasn't eaten anything. You're still nauseous, honey, aren't you?"

A grimace passed over Clare's face. "My mouth's got a horrible taste in it, like sulfur or some weird metal or something."

"It's her kidneys, isn't it?" Boon looked at Zoe, panicked.

Zoe didn't want to scare him any more than he already was, but there was no way to sugarcoat the pill. She ran a hand through her wet, tangled hair and tried to figure out what to say.

Clare turned in Boon's arms and looked up at him. "You know I haven't been well, hon. That's why I came to Sol. I hoped he could cure me, but he couldn't, and I've been feeling worse." She sighed and leaned back against Boon's shoulder again, closing her eyes. A deep sadness came over her face. "My kidneys are failing."

Relief washed over Zoe. After all the arguments and all the disputes, it was huge for Clare to say the words. She was finally moving out of denial.

"Are you going to die?" Boon looked terrified.

Clare shook her head but stayed silent. Tears were running down her face.

Zoe spoke up. "She's going to need to go on dialysis, or—"

"Dialys—what?" Boon stared at her blankly. It was obvious he'd never heard the word before.

"Dialysis," she repeated, enunciating each syllable. "If

your kidneys don't work, you'll die, because your body can't balance its chemistry and get rid of toxins. Dialysis takes the place of your kidneys and can keep you alive."

"But Clare's not on dialysis. Is she going to die?" Boon sank to the ground, hugging Clare close.

"Not if I can help it," Zoe said. "I'll see if one of those police trucks can take her to a hospital."

She looked down the convoy of vehicles but didn't see where Jason had taken Heller. She hurried over to the big van at the front. The man slid down the window again when she reached it.

"Do you have a medical unit? My sister needs a doctor."

The man was big and bald and looked more like a thug than a police officer. He studied her with narrowed eyes and then squinted beyond her to where Boon sat on the ground with Clare.

"Check two units back. They've got a medic." The man gestured with his thumb.

She thanked him and hurried past the van and a black SUV to another black SUV. The back doors were open. Heller was being examined and several other men were preparing to unload a stretcher with a body on it.

"Are any of you doctors?" she asked.

"I'm an EMT," one of the men said.

"My sister needs help, quickly. Can you take a look at her?"

"Sure, but just a minute," the EMT said.

Zoe watched impatiently as they slid the stretcher with the man on it out of the SUV, popped down the stretcher's wheels, and hooked the two IV bags feeding into the man's forearm up to an IV pole. She looked down at the man with surprise. It was Derrick Hanks.

"He's not dead, is he?"

"He's alive, but in bad shape. We're doing what we can to stabilize him," the EMT said. "The medevac helicopter should be here any moment."

As if on cue, the distant thump-thump of propellers grew quickly louder, until the roar obliterated all else. The helicopter's landing light flicked on. The beam sliced through the twilight and illuminated a spot in the parking area. The helicopter hovered, then slowly descended and touched down, the roar of its engine lessening as the rotor blades slowed. The side door opened and a man climbed out, keeping his head lowered below the rotating blades. He walked over to them.

"What have we got?" he said.

While the one man discussed Hanks with the doctor, the EMT turned to Zoe. "Let's have a look at your sister."

As Zoe led him over to Clare and Boon, she explained, "She's got chronic kidney disease, but I think her kidneys are failing. She's got all the symptoms, the nausea, extreme pallor, uremia." Sadness filled her that Clare's health had come to this.

The EMT crouched beside her sister. "I'm an Emergency Medical Technician. Do you mind if I take your pulse?"

Clare gave him a weak smile and extended a limp hand from under the blanket. Boon held her other hand, his face drawn and worried. The EMT performed a quick exam, checked her vitals, and then stood up, his expression grim.

"We have to get her to the hospital," he said to Zoe and Boon. "I'll see if we can get her on the chopper. You OK with that?"

"Yes, please," Zoe nodded fervently. Thank God, Clare was going to finally get help!

The man hurried away. Boon hugged Clare close against his side. Clare opened her eyes and looked up at Zoe. There were tears in them.

"I'm sorry I've made everything so hard for you," she said.

"No apology needed, but if it makes you feel better, I accept." Zoe swiped tears from her own eyes and smiled, trying to lighten the moment.

The EMT came back with the other man and the stretcher, and Zoe sighed with relief. There'd be no delay in getting Clare treatment. Boon hovered beside the men as they helped Clare onto the stretcher. He wouldn't let go of Clare's hand, his face desperate.

"Please, can I go with her?" he asked.

"The chopper's got a weight limit, but it may be possible. Let me check with the pilot," the EMT said as they wheeled Clare away.

"Do you mind?" Boon turned to Zoe, tears in his eyes. "I need to be with her, but you're her sister—"

"You love her, Boon. Go, and take good care of her," Zoe said.

"I will, I promise." Boon gave her a quick hug and then dashed after Clare.

Zoe spotted Jason over by the medical SUV with Heller, who was being examined by the EMT. Jason caught her eye. He said a few words to the EMT and then came over. Zoe's heartbeat kicked up a beat.

"Hey there," he said when he reached her.

She pulled him to her and hugged him tight. She felt awash on a sea of emotion. The ordeal and her adventure in Humboldt was finally coming to an end. She took a deep breath and then exhaled, letting it all go.

Jason stroked her back and she relaxed into his comforting, solid strength. He smelled of wood smoke and patchouli and Jason. Together, they watched Clare being loaded onto the helicopter with Boon hovering alongside.

The EMT came back and handed a card to Zoe. "Here's the contact info for the medevac service. We'll transport your sister to the community hospital in Garberville. You'll be able to arrange further transport from there."

"Thanks." She took the card from him.

"You OK?" Jason asked when the EMT left.

"Just tired," she said, feeling her arm ache where Heller had shot her. After everything she'd been through, she was thoroughly exhausted.

The helicopter started up again and the place echoed with its chopping roar. They watched the helicopter lift off and disappear over the trees. A few stars twinkled overhead in the night sky. Jason stroked her back one last time and then released her.

"Let's catch a ride to Garberville," he said, taking her hand.

"I'm so glad we don't have to hike there!" she laughed.

Together, they walked to the convoy that was starting to move down the mountain.

***

CHAPTER EIGHTEEN

One month later, October, San Francisco

On a Friday evening in October, Zoe jogged beside Jason on the wet sand of Baker Beach, just beyond the reach of the crashing surf. The sun sank low over the slate-blue line of the Pacific. North across the water, the Marin Headlands rose dark and dramatic, and to the northeast, the Golden Gate Bridge glowed red. A fully laden container ship chugged beneath the bridge's lengthy center span, bound for the Port of Oakland.

"I love San Francisco!" Zoe said as she drank in the view. "The City's so crowded, and yet, in just a few miles—isn't this amazing?"

She spread her arms wide and felt the whisper-light warmth of the evening sun on her skin. Her heart filled with joy to be with Jason again.

"Breathtaking," he said, watching her.

She ran with an easy, carefree stride, her face radiant in the glow of the setting sun. Tonight, they were finally going to have their first real dinner date. She smiled at him, and he felt all the tension that had kept him wound tight the past month release. He took a deep breath of the moist marine air, let it out, and grinned back at her.

"I'm so glad we're finally getting together," she said. "Work's been insane, and with my sister and Boon crashing at my apartment, this is the first downtime I've had."

"Same here," he said, speeding up to avoid an incoming wave.

She sprinted after him. When they slowed back to a jog again, he continued, "I finished the paperwork on the Humboldt case this week. Now that Heller's all patched up, you'll be happy to hear he's in jail awaiting trial."

"Good riddance, but with him gone, won't someone else take his place?" She remembered all the dangerous-looking men with guns at the pot harvest.

"Probably, but that's why I do my job. Somebody's gotta fight for what's right."

"I can't imagine taking on that battle. You're a better person than I am."

"I've seen what kind of person you are," he said, remembering her tenacity and courage, braving the hardships of the Humboldt redwoods in her quest to find her sister. He'd talked on the phone with her a few times since they'd left Humboldt, but he hadn't heard all the details of her sister's transplant. "How're Clare and Boon doing now?"

"No sign of rejection, thank goodness, and Boon's in good shape, too. They've been out of the hospital for two weeks and Clare's doing so well now. She's sore from the operation, but besides that, she says she feels better than she has in a very long time. The big news is that they're getting married."

"Aren't they kind of young?"

"Definitely, but Boon landed a job in Seattle that has great health insurance. Turns out he's a brewmaster.

They're moving this weekend." Zoe still couldn't believe the whirlwind events of the past month. Clare had a new lease on a healthy life, and she was getting married! Zoe felt a surge of unfamiliar and welcome freedom.

"So they're leaving the Seekers?" Jason asked.

"Clare told me that once Sol's released, he's planning to move what's left of the Seekers to Oregon where they can escape the drought and find a better environment for their plants. I'm sure he wants to keep it all legal, too, after what happened." Zoe shrugged as she ran, imagining Sol finding another forest and another group of young, eager people looking for a father figure and easy answers to their life problems. She was just glad her sister had moved on.

"Clare and Boon don't need Sol or the Seekers anymore. They've found each other," she said.

Jason reached out and took Zoe's hand as a flock of gulls wheeled overhead.

"And me, you," he said.

They slowed to a stop and she moved into his arms. They stood at the water's edge and watched the sunset.

"Not like the last sunset we watched at the black sand beach, is it?" she said, remembering that strange night of Sol's harvest moon ritual on the Lost Coast.

"I like this sunset better." He held her closer. "But I'd like to go back there sometime with you, under different circumstances, of course," he chuckled.

Images of ancient forests and quiet tree cathedrals moved through her mind. "I'd like that, and I'd love to visit the old-growth redwoods again. You grew up in an amazing place."

She admired the shifting change in color as the sky washed red above where the sun sank into the shimmering steel of the ocean. She sighed. "California is so beautiful."

He rubbed his cheek against her hair. He'd forgotten how good she smelled. "You are, too."

She pivoted in his arms, still surprised at how different he looked without his Seeker disguise and how much better looking. She stroked her hand along his clean-shaven jaw, its strong line revealed now that the shaggy beard was gone.

"You clean up well, yourself," she grinned, giving into temptation. She stood on tiptoe to land a light kiss on his mouth.

As he looked down at her, he couldn't help remembering the night they spent together in the cabin. "I missed you."

"I missed kissing you." She smiled. Anticipation shimmered through her at the desire growing in his eyes.

"I need to refresh my memory," he grinned.

The kiss was long and deep and passionate and filled with possibility.

When they finally pulled apart, the sun had set. A cool breeze began to blow.

"How about a hot shower?" he suggested as they started to jog again toward the stairs that led up from the beach. "My roommate is out of town on a business trip and I've got the whole place to myself."

"I'll race you!" Zoe dashed forward, taking the lead up the steep log stairs.

Jason followed in hot pursuit and caught her at the Baker Beach parking lot. They stopped, side by side, laughing as they caught their breaths.

Behind them lay the vast Pacific Ocean and their separate personal histories. They moved together toward a shared future. As they entered the Presidio, their strides lengthened. They glanced at each other. Laughing again, they broke into a run.

THE END

###

ACKNOWLEDGMENTS

Many thanks to my friends at the Woodside Writers Group: Hillary Avis, Elizabeth Fergason, Jenness Hobart, Staci Homrig, and Debbie Romani for their invaluable advice. Special thanks to my long time friend and writing compatriot Rebecca Douglass for help with both early and final drafts. And last but never least, thanks to my family: Lila for your enthusiasm and Kurt, who makes this all possible.

ABOUT THE AUTHOR

Lisa Frieden grew up in California and spent a few unforgettable years in Santa Barbara. She's read everything from William Shakespeare to Elizabeth Lowell and relishes romantic suspense, in which she finds the perfect combination of love, mystery, and suspense to shape her own storytelling. She lives, loves, dreams, and writes in the Bay Area. www.friedenpress.com.

BOOKS BY LISA FRIEDEN

Finding Clarity

The Offering

Dialysis: a Memoir